VIA Folios 117

My Three Sicilies

Stories, Poems, and Histories

Joseph A. Amato

Library of Congress Control Number: 2015949496

COVER ART
Felice Amato
Artist and Author's Daughter
Melancholy, 2011
(Fired terracotta and Wire)

COVER DESIGN
Marcy D. Olson

Printed in the United States.

Published by
BORDIGHERA PRESS
John D. Calandra Italian American Institute
25 West 43rd Street, 17th Floor
New York, NY 10036

VIA FOLIOS 117
ISBN 978-1-59954-095-5

TABLE OF CONTENTS

PART THREE
Essay

ACKNOWLEDGMENTS

My Three Sicilies arose from a Sicilian-American family, the family that gave me a distinct sense of spirit and flesh and ever evokes my memory and gratitude. Its persons, immigrations, and experience in the 1930s, 40s, and 50s joined me to the working class of east side Detroit, which around an oak dining-room table, on factory floors, and then on European battlefields made us Sicilian-Americans. That family formed a place, a time, and half a world, so contrasted and matched by my mother's mixed Prussian, Irish, English, and Acadian rural Wisconsin and urban Detroit family.

My Sicilian family is given its history and life in the Part Three "Essay" of this work. It was published in an earlier version as the first chapter of *Jacob's Well: A Case for Rethinking Family History* by the Minnesota Historical Society Press in 2008. I acknowledge the memories and anecdotes of my mother, Ethel May, and my father, Joseph, with additions from cousins Angie and RoseMarie and the tenacious genealogical work of cousin John (Amato) Notaro on display on his website "Sicilian Genealogy & Family Research," which offers guides to ours and a number of other Sicilian families and their hometowns in Sicily (https://web.archive.org/web/20090518013213/http://home.roadrunner.com/~siciliani/).

Part One of this work, "Stories," my first experiment in short stories, is an imaginative sketch of relatives and neighbors known in Detroit, Pennsylvania, and Sicily. It is, above all, a projection of the difficult life of my most faithful and passionate grandmother Rosalia, to whom this work is dedicated. She suffered the early, sudden, and tragic death of her husband Antonino in October 1915. They had just begun their march into America when *la miseria* caught up and dealt a black hand of spades to Rosalia, only twenty-seven. She was left alone with my three-year-old father and pregnant with his sister Epiphania and a long hard road to follow despite the help of relatives and fellow Sicilian villagers.

In transforming the Sicilian and American lives and migrations of Rosalia and Antonino into these short stories, my flame, forge, and anvil were Verga, Silone, and Lampedusa. I am indebted to Frank Polizzi, editor of the Irish-Mediterranean *Feile-Festa* for the publication of the first story, "Augurina," in its Spring 2015 issue.

None of the three parts of this work, fiction, poetry, and prose could have been written without long years of study that grafted me, both spirit and memory, to a joint Italian and Sicilian identity. I reduce to only a handful of acknowledgments what became ways of thinking, hoping, and praying. All three grandparents I knew—Rosalia, German-Irish William Linsdau, and his Francis (Boudrot) Linsdau—were European and North American country folk and storytellers. They fostered my interest in myth, folklore, and worldviews, which were supplied with validation and reading lists by historiographer Stephen Tonsor at the University of Michigan and French-Canadian ethnographer and folklorist Luc Lacourcière at the Université de Laval.

With advanced graduate study at the University of Rochester came the gift of having Professor A. W. Salomone, dramatic dialectician of nineteenth-century Europe, as teacher and sponsor of my dissertation on French Catholic thought. As I studied medieval and Renaissance Italy, Salomone awakened and molded my first interest in modern Italian history, politics, and culture. With my study of modern Italy, as was nearly inevitable, came an irrepressible and insatiable interest in the land of the Italian south, the Mezzogiorno, and especially Sicily.

My first trip to Sicily in the early 1970s was not taken to restore ties with a long lost family. Instead, I went to meet Danilo Dolci, a nonviolent social reformer, whom the French heralded as the Gandhi of Sicily and I took to be my Cesar Chavez. President of "Friends of Danilo Dolci," sociologist Alfred McClung Lee generously invited me to his home as did Sicilian-American writer Jerre Mangione, whose 1968 biography *The World Around Danilo Dolci* filled out and complemented my knowledge of Dolci and whose stirring 1940 classic *Mount Allegro*, depicting his own migration to Rochester, New York, authenticated the value of thinking of writing about the experience of my family on the east side of Detroit. I gave first form to this thought in my 1976 "Parents and Grandparents: We Are All Immigrants and Migrants" (*Great Lakes Review*, Winter, 1976).

Dolci, along with his staff, including Mafia researcher Franco Alasia and Italian-American educator Leonardo Covello visiting from New York, welcomed me to their centers at Partinico and Trapetto. They chauffeured me around southwestern Sicily—to visit Bellice Valley, which had been stricken by an earthquake in 1968; slums in Palermo; a new wine co-op in Trapani—and even took me to a labor demonstration in central Palermo. In turn, I hosted Danilo Dolci at our small college in southwestern Minnesota on his Fall 1972 tour of the United States. I consolidated my understanding and praise of Dolci under two rubrics expressed by the titles of two essays, "A Poetic Modernizer" (*Worldview*, 1973) and "A Nonviolent Reformer" (*Italian Americana*, 1978).

Additional trips to Italy and Sicily were prepared for with intense study of Italian and intermittent reading of Sicilian poetry (found in *Arba Sicula* and elsewhere) and Sicilian history, with a special appreciation of folktales and proverbs, and assimilated afterward by the inner crafting of memory of family and youth into foundational essays and elemental poetry. Ever more consciously I absorbed the past—in memory, tradition, history, and language—to root and express myself in the living present. Meantime, an ongoing discussion with two friends and Minnesotans, Rudolph Vecoli, founder and director of the Immigrant Archives at the University of Minnesota, and Thaddeus Radzilowski, long-time friend, colleague, scholar of American ethnicity, and founder and president of PIAST, National Institute for Polish and Polish American Affairs, educated me in the power of ethnicity in defining American experience and led me on behalf of family, place, region, and peasantry to take sides against class, race, and official national identities. I started saying and continue to say, "The variety of the past is greater than the diversity of the present."

Subsequent trips to Sicily were highlighted by enriching and rooting visits to Rosalia's welcoming Notaro relatives in Montemaggiore Belsito, and the hospitality of Antonino's Cerda and ever-generous grandniece and husband Francesca and Franco Di Blasi, who shared garden, food, and stories with my wife and me. My most recent trip to Sicily in May 2014 had a different sponsor and purpose. It was generously funded by the Southwest Minnesota Humanities Commission for the writing of poetry, which resulted in Part Two: "Poems."

My itinerary started with day trips in and out of Palermo, Cefalù, and Enna, which accounted for the majority of poems on landscape, sites, and flora. Others poems on place and countryside resulted from hooking up for six days with founder Damian Croft's Esplora group, which sponsored an educational and walking tour of the Madonie Mountains, a vast land of valley and forest just to the east of Grandmother and Grandfather's upland agricultural villages.

Sicilian poet, writer, and philosopher Cateno Tempio invited me to give an informal talk in his hometown Regalbuto. He initiated our growing correspondence with a review of the second edition of my book *Dust: A History of the Small and Invisible, Polvere: La Storia del piccolo e dell invisible* on "SitoSophia" (http://www.sitosophia.org) and later translated the two poems on Enna in this volume on his website, "Due inediti siciliani di Joseph A. Amato" (http://www.riversopoesia.it/due-inediti-siciliani-di-joseph -a-amato-trad-di-cateno-tempio/).

In advance of my trip, Sicilian philosopher Silvia Bellia introduced *Polvere* to the readers of her website (http://www.hounlibrointesta.it/autore /silvia-bellia/page/2/) and set up appointments with Cateno Tempio and teacher and writer Michele Burgio. Along with wife and child, Michele hosted me for an evening in Palermo.

The trip produced in draft a poem or two a day, for a grand total of thirty-poems, which I supplemented with other new and older poems on family. A handful came from my recent collection of poems, *Buoyancies: A Ballast Master's Log* (Spoon River Poetry Press/Crossings Press, 2014) and one poem, "A Sicilian Father," was added from my *Death Book: Terrors, Consolations, Contradictions, and Paradoxes* (Ellis Press, 1985). *A Sicilian Father* was first translated and published into Italian by New York Sicilian American Nat Scammaca.

Finally, I need to express my gratitude to several individuals. Poet and writer Dana Yost is a wonderful and trusted source of encouragement and criticism. Poet and translator Michael Palma, as poetry editor of *Italian*

Americana, sharpened my craft. Most keen and imaginative copyeditor, writer and poet Suzanne Noguere improved the entire work and wrote its Preface. Professor, writer, editor, and co-founder Anthony Julian Tamburri welcomed the work to Bordighera Press and thoughtfully husbanded it through publication. My daughter Felice's sculpture Melancholy, 2011, of fired terracotta and wire, furnished the art for the cover of the work, which Marcy Olson, publications editor at Southwest Minnesota, Marshall, Minnesota, brought to such pleasing form. And then there is my abiding wife, Catherine, whose love and patience sustain my seemingly endless attempts to harvest meanings with words.

PREFACE

Ennius, poet of ancient Rome, said that he had three hearts because he spoke three languages—Latin, Oscan, and Greek. It is a claim that we could make for Joseph Amato in *My Three Sicilies* as he speaks to us—fluently and *sui generis*—in the three languages of fiction, poetry, and history. Three hearts are the minimum Amato needs to hold the memories and feelings that have fueled his lifelong development of a Sicilian-American identity in coming to understand his heritage.

In America, the great melting pot, it is not unusual for one's genealogy to encompass a diversity of national origins, cultures, and ethnicities. And in this land of opportunity, one particular opportunity is the choice of which part or parts of that ancestry to claim as truly one's own: which is central and which peripheral. Though I suspect that Amato has made the entire mix a way of knowing the world and defining the self, here—as the only son of an only son and now keeper of the graves—he follows his love for his Sicilian grandmother, Rosalia, and seeks somehow to encounter the Sicilian grandfather he never knew, Antonino, who died at thirty-three, leaving Rosalia a young widow in Detroit with one child by her side and another on the way.

The longing to know what Rosalia's and Antonino's lives were like before coming to America leads Amato to transcend the grandparent-grandchild relationship and write as if he were their contemporary. Thus begin four interlocking short stories—each focused on an unforgettable character: two on strong indomitable women and two on deeply sympathetic men struggling to find their way in a hostile world.

The first story, "Augurina," brings alive its remarkable heroine, Anna Tasca Ventimiglia, who arrives in a poor mountain village in northwestern Sicily as a mysterious stranger with her young daughter, Angelina. Excited by Anna's beauty, suspicious of her circumstances, intrigued by her industry, the villagers gradually come to accept and then rely upon her, according her unusual respect for her powers of healing and fortune telling. But the one fortune she cannot tell is her own. Hardship returns, and when relatives in America send tickets for Anna and Angelina to emigrate, there is only one decision to make: Angelina must go. There is no future here.

In the second story, "La Destinata," Angelina, nineteen years old and the spitting image of her mother, has emigrated alone to Kelayres in the Pennsylvania anthracite region to join her aunt and uncle. Here is an immigrant community, heavily Sicilian, centered on church and work in the coal mines for the men. Angelina herself works for five years cleaning houses and cooking to save money in order to bring her beau and betrothed, Vincenzu, to America. The entire village of Kelayres comes to know her story and palpably feel the bitter fury she vents against the church's patron saint, San Mauru, when Vincenzu arrives from Sicily mortally ill.

"Flight into the Elements" is Vincenzu's own story of trying to reach America and Angelina. Unexpectedly on the run after a fatal fight with two men who failed to pay for his family's artichokes, Vincenzu makes his way through hard terrain to the seaside cathedral of Cefalù, where an old friend teaches in the seminary. That priest befriends him, leading eventually to work helping a geologist-priest collect and haul rock specimens in the mountains. The priest's glorification of rocks becomes anathema to Vincenzu, but their agreement is that in four months Vincenzu will board a ship in Palermo and set sail for America. That does indeed happen, but Vincenzu boards with the priest's help, without its being noticed how sick he is.

"War of the Saints" is the story of Angelina's son, Antonino, first-generation American, who studies in Rome and visits her old home in Sicily as a young priest, feeling a deep connection. Upon his return to the United States, his first ministry is Kelayres itself. Many Neapolitans have since settled there, and on the very day that Antonino arrives a fierce rivalry has broken out between the Neapolitans and the Sicilians about the status of their respective saints—San Gennaro and San Mauru. Young Antonino is called upon to mediate, and though his decision is fair, no one is pleased with it or him. His loneliness opens him to the false hospitality and confidence of Joseph Bruno, a neighbor who ultimately reveals himself to be a corrupt power broker.

In these four compelling stories Amato has not only created characters to cherish but re-created communities, landscapes, worldviews, and the immigrant experience over three generations spanning the last three decades of the nineteenth century and the first four of the twentieth.

In Part Two, the poems, Amato speaks in his own voice as a second-generation American intent on continuity and honoring the grandparents who made his life possible. It is a theme he touched on in his fine first collection of poems, *Buoyancies: A Ballast Master's Log*. While we can imagine that it is Amato's lifelong profession as historian and his study of literature that have turned him into a master storyteller, I think it is his depth of feeling and love of language that have transformed him into a poet as well. Occasioned by visits to Sicily, the poems here are those of an acutely observant traveler trying to see what his ancestors saw, to inhabit not just their place but their experience. He is the traveler who is also intensely seeking himself, the life he might have had, the landscape that might have been home. At the same time, the poems bring life in America into focus. We learn what America held in store for his grandmother Rosalia and her family.

One would think at this point that all has been spoken, but Part Three opens another dimension. Part memoir, part history, it grounds all that we've read in the harsh light and hard facts of history, especially the over-population and unrelenting poverty and policies that drove rural Europeans, and specifically southern Italians and Sicilians, to the United States, Canada, and Latin America throughout the twentieth century. We learn as well that the tragic deaths in "War of the Saints" were not fictional but all too real: they occurred in the largely unreported Kelayres Massacre in 1934. Beyond that, the essay documents Amato's intellectual awakening and the key role that being Rosalia's grandson had in his development as a historian with a deep, abiding interest in peasants the world over, particularly nineteenth- and twentieth-century European peasantry, an interest that has extended into scholarly work on the rural life around him in Minnesota. It is now the attainment of age, of being the oldest generation himself and memorialist by spirit that gives Amato's history its urgency, as he seeks simultaneously to document and commemorate the fortitude of his grandparents, a testament to both the Sicilian and American experiences.

There is an arresting portrait of King Charles I by Van Dyck, sometimes titled "Charles I in Three Positions." Dead center is a grave frontal portrait of the standing king, visible to the waist. Next to him on the left, he stands in full profile in a differently colored costume. Next to him on the right, he stands in three-quarter profile, again differently arrayed. This magnetic portrait had a most pragmatic aim: to allow Bernini to sculpt Charles in 3D from afar without ever having seen him in person—in which aim it proved entirely successful. Pragmatism of technique aside, there hovers about the portrait the expectation that Charles is about to engage in conversation with himself. In *My Three Sicilies* Amato has that conversation with himself, and Sicily comes alive in every dimension.

Suzanne Noguere

PART ONE

Stories

AUGURINA

She appeared one afternoon on Montemaggiore's piazza. She had a suitcase in one hand, held a young girl with the other. Not one of the old men gathered on the square had any idea where she came from or what she was about.

Like a freshly opened faucet, they stuttered and stammered and blurted out ideas until a full and rushing conversation got underway. Cruciano Notaro started things off saying, more in jest than true conjecture, that she was the bandit daughter of Antonio La Rosa, while Cruciano's neighbor, Paul De Carlo, proposed that she was another bastard daughter of the local prince who considered Italian unification as a reason to join in solidarity with every citizen who wore a skirt.

All laughed when jokester Giuseppe Cucuzza claimed she was from Cacca di Lupo, which was no specific place at all. It was simply anywhere outside of town where the wolf chooses to shit. When they asked him exactly where Cacca di Lupo was he said down the road near Caccamo. Most agreed at the end of an hour's speculation that she came into town from the north, which meant either the southern fork that led up onto a plain leading to Agrigento or the eastern fork that led into the higher reaches of the Madonie.

Of course, conversations sloshed out of the piazza into homes, and evening conversations only flooded back the next day when she took up residence in a small shed on the outskirts of town in a small garden abandoned for three seasons after widow Serafina Tocco, the town witch, died.

Swirling and eddying pockets of gossip asked: Was this newcomer, with child and airs, the secret daughter of *Strega Tocco*? And if so, did she have powers to bewitch the town? Surely *Strega Tocco*, all chimed in, rivaled the priest and the schoolteacher as an authority on coincidences, happenings, and coming events. Indeed, beyond offering an explanation for every mishap and tragedy, as did the priest with his stable of saints and the schoolteachers with blackboards of statistics about progress, *Strega Tocco* was taken to be source and cause of every odd happening, be it an unexpected death, a mudslide, or a hailstorm. Surely in the village mind the newcomer's potency rivaled that of the government in Rome and the diverse miracles of Saint Anthony. Santa Rosalia still ruled as queen of pity and mercy.

Prejudice grew, spontaneously in some and grudgingly in others, as weeks went by and this woman-from-afar neither violently looked away from others nor stared deeply at them as if to steal their souls. Indeed, as she bought and paid for her bread, milk, vegetables, and meat, she went about town with a pleasant demeanor. She enrolled her daughter in school and demanded no special provisions or treatment. She signed their names on the school roster, Anna Tasca Ventimiglia and Angelina, her daughter, who had just turned seven.

Her name, Anna Tasca Ventimiglia, allowed the postmaster, the town's largest gossip, to use every letter she received and sent to move the mills of suspicion. He made what hay he could out of one letter to and from America; unfortunately no one, except a few know-it-alls, even had an idea about Pennsylvania. And neither the postmaster nor the villagers could connect her name to any place in Sicily they knew. Of course, only a handful had ever been more than fifteen kilometers from the village.

She allayed much suspicion with the currency peasants knew counted most: unlike Strega Tocco she worked without cease, and she worked not with words, spells, and telling numbers, but with her hands. She tilled her garden, repaired and painted the shed. In fact, the praise she received for her combination of work and beauty from the village's men aroused the jealousy of their hardworking wives. Always at the extreme, Rosalia Battimani let loose her anger by splashing some boiling pasta on her husband's lap the third time he praised Signora Anna Tasca Ventimiglia, saying, "This ought to sizzle your sausage! You Boccione-Fanulla!"

Granting grounds for the suspicious, Anna didn't go to church on Sunday. She spent much of the Sabbath sitting on an old cane chair, reading, while encouraging her daughter to draw and write. She did this while embroidered sheets and pillowcases flapped on her clothesline. "A *cafone* during the week, a *burgisi* on Sunday," said jester Cucuzza.

But above all else, her striking appearance continued to command the attention of the village. She was a head taller than the average woman. Her hair, as black as the deepest sea on a moonless and starless night, was accented by her ivory skin, which made them all say, "She is no Arab, but she is a true Greek—non '*raba ma vera greca*.'" Her eyes, sparkling black, were covered by long and thin eyebrows; her long and sharp nose and chin were complemented by her small and sharp breasts, small waist and ample hips, which tapered to long and thin ankles. Angular, like a *marchese*, constant energy poured out of her. Lighter and more graceful than other women, she walked as if she were above the earth she tread, as if she would simply float up and away one day. If she weren't a witch, she was a misplaced spirit.

Yet, as tugged at the mind of village, she had a daughter and no husband. What the men couldn't fathom was the idea that she slept alone. "Obviously, she has danced before," Cucuzza said, "and once you do this dance," he elaborated, "it's hard to keep your feet on the floor." Every male, if only to save his image, declared how much he would like to dance with her. The women all assented to the truth that daughter Angelina was the spitting image of the mother and formed a chorus, ending every line with the refrain, "*Strega Anna* ain't Santa Maria and doesn't even have a Saint Giuseppe."

Powerless before the weather, disease, a curse, or the kick of the family mule, all the villagers fused Anna to their superstitious minds, except the town's two fatalists. Antonio Bevacqua proclaimed that witches and saints "are *imputenti* when it comes to the future. The future comes in two forms—one that we must endure and the other that kills us off." He always added, the woes of tomorrow suffice without worrying about tomorrow.

Carlo Marteddu, the local blacksmith, articulated a more cosmological case for resignation. With large biceps complementing his authority, Carlo pounded out his opinions as if he were beating a white-hot horseshoe on his anvil. "Look at the stars above. They have a great design but we cannot figure it out. Plans up there are too great for understanding down here. God guarantees nothing, neither a long life nor an easy death. He only assures us work." And then, he invariably summed up his philosophizing as if he were speaking to himself by saying, "So keep your head down. Keep pounding. And make sparks fly."

Even though the majority conceded for the moment the truth of what Carlo said, they picked and pried at the meaning of every odd thing that came their way to find out what was in store for them. Furthermore, omens abounded and portended. Signs of death clustered everywhere, and one could bring bad luck so many ways. Even sweeping all the dust out of one's house might open the door to bad spirits. Day witnessed strange messengers of bad news: a bird perching on the window or, worse, a sure sign of death, a bird flying into a house. Night brought the mournful hooting of an owl, the baying of a dog, and dreams of weddings and children telling of their opposite, death.

The wearing of amulets around their necks, the hanging of garlic and pictures of saints in their homes, the sprinkling of salt on the threshold, or the hanging of bright horns over one's front door could not keep evil at bay.

Anna knew gossip's wagging tongue. She didn't need to be reminded that people and donkeys are the same wherever you find them. Already ostracized in her home village, how could she, a stranger and unmarried mother, living in the shed and garden of the witch on the outskirts of town, expect not to fall under dark clouds in Montemaggiore Belsito?

When Ziu Sebastianu wrote from Pennsylvania giving her permanent use of his dead sister's garden in Montemaggiore, Anna knew she would be considered the new snake in it. But still she didn't hesitate a second to accept his and Paulina's offer after everything she had experienced in the last seven years since her father, the lord and doctor of La Valle dell' Olmo, had banished her from her home to a shack at the back of the family estate. Their offer came as the first flicker of hope in a long dark tunnel since she had been raped by a cousin and responded by categorically refusing to marry him and chose not to have an abortion. She ferociously stood her ground, even after the young count beseeched her in public to marry him and her father publicly consented to the marriage. Her defiance poured out of her eyes and flowed from every gesture her graceful body made. She truly was *mafiusa*.

Up to the night of the rape, the world had been hers. Fickle *fortuna* smiled on her. The oldest and favorite child of the town's doctor, she was handsome, intelligent, and, most important of all, spirited. In school there was no subject at which she did not shine, but she was keenest at mathematics, the natural sciences, and drawing.

Called *Leonarda* in the Valle dell' Olmo, she took to her father's profession better than any imagined son could have. She especially enjoyed doing his autopsies. She showed the finesse of an experienced hand with her father's new stainless knives and instruments. It was expected by all—teachers, parents, and villagers—that she would go to the University of Palermo and study medicine, an expectation she was on the eve of fulfilling when the rape occurred.

In fact, the night Anna was violated she was descending from her father's stable above town. She had spent the whole day there dissecting and drawing the parts of a dead horse her father had given her as a gift for her eighteenth birthday. Fascinated by the valves and muscle tissue of the horse's heart, she stayed on drawing that night under the flickering light of the lantern.

No sooner did she leave the stable than her cousin approached her and tried out a few clumsy memorized romantic praises. When she didn't respond, he pounced on her. Tall and strong, he overwhelmed her. First she was paralyzed by surprise and finally subdued by his protracted force. She bit and clawed him, as scratches on his face, neck, and ears testified. No one doubted that if she had not left her knife in the stable, she would have cut him to ribbons.

He knew that he would have to rape her to have her. No one who had ever been in their presence was unaware that as he was attracted to her, so she was repulsed by him. The more he pushed himself toward her, the more she retreated. Like magnets—"*come magneti,*" remarked Benedettu Semplica. "His eyes clung to her like prickers to pants." Her indifference to him only heated his desire to have her. The idea that she did not find him—tall, blond, and rich—attractive made him crazy with anger. His whole body yearned for her more and more as the day of departure for the university drew closer and closer. The one time he had gathered courage to ask her father's permission to court her, she trumped her father's tentative yes with an emphatic no.

After the rape, he did everything he could to win her over. Some said it was then he went mad. He frequently got publicly drunk and went around town saying that one day she would truly love him. He sent her flowers, messages, and a raft of plagiarized poems. His complexion grew more ashen as her refusal grew with each day more certain. With her pregnancy showing, which she did not disguise, he killed himself with his shotgun. As a punishment for failing to marry and shaming her family, Anna was exiled to live in the stable where she had performed her autopsies.

Knowing nothing of all this in Montemaggiore, the villagers waited for her powers, whatever they might be, to manifest themselves. She was like a sky auguring a storm, a wind-swept landscape announcing a coming drama. But nothing dramatic broke forth. Rather, trepidations were tamped down by her benign and humble actions. She cured a neighbor's wheezing donkey by feeding him a special mixture of plants. She stopped the profuse bleeding of a child with compacts, a splint, and a few stitches. She set the foot of another child, who suffered a compound fracture of the ankle, when no doctor was available. Upon later seeing her work, he openly confessed he could have done no better. She helped new mothers learn to nurse their babies by putting honey on their nipples. She encouraged one mother to put a bonnet on her jaundiced baby and set it in the sunlight for half an hour every day. The baby's eventual beautiful complexion shined with a testimony to Anna's good powers.

Soon, on Sunday afternoons, individuals in need of help formed a steady stream between village and her shack. Anna was required to add a few chairs to her small patio—and, with a rope and a few posts, she staked out a waiting area adjacent to the garden for her clients. Benedettu declared, "Witch or not, she is as busy as the priest during Easter season." When individuals from other villages began to make Sunday pilgrimages to her, local people began to count her cures as miracles. The curious began to hang around her shack just to see and hear what cures she might perform. She did little in her garden that wasn't almost immediately on the town square.

With more people came a parade of human somatic and mental maladies. One supplicant worried about the effects of a curse on his daughter. Another worried about a mysterious disease among his chickens, while yet a third had suffered constipation for almost a month. One father came worried about the imminent military conscription of his only son. A young woman pregnant for the first time wondered about the screaming she heard from the child within her womb.

Anna first asked her clients and petitioners to make an offering—a sum of money, a few coins, a chicken or two, a bag of fennel, or some olive oil—or at least say a prayer for her. Then she had her clients tell their stories twice, once without interrupting them. She allowed them to pour out their pent-up emotions, fears, and wishes. The second time she forced them to slow down and directly, slowly, and methodically, to describe their conditions, wants, and fears as precisely as they could.

Unwittingly at first and then as a conscious system, she began to classify her clients, whose condition was usually revealed by posture, gesture, eyes, first words, or tone of voice. First, and easiest to deal with, there were those who needed a few encouraging words—*pocu curaggiu*—or basic treatment with simple home remedies of teas, herbs, and dietary regimes. Some of their group were often treated best with a proverb or joke. Her favorite curing phrase, always worth a smile, was "*Cu'mancia, fa caca.*" ("Who eats, shits.")

To cheer up her women in their endless duties, she repeated pure old sayings as "Every nose fits its face" ("*Ogni nosu sta bedeu a so facci"*) and "The wife makes or destroys the home" (*"A femmina fa, o disfa, la casa"*). At the other extreme stood her most difficult cases, which she called to herself *i casi mali di male*; they included cases of the *malaffurtunati* and *malagguriu* (the misfortunate and ill-omened), and then the *malanimu, malavogghia, malcontentu,* and *malancuniusu,* that is the bad spirited, the nasty willed, the discontented, and the melancholy. There were those who in despair would suck the energy from her and all those around them.

In turn, there were the abandoned, mutilated, crippled, truly ugly, and the dying. They suffered what no one could repair. She listened to their tales of woe only once, allowing them to cry and curse as much as they wished on the way to completing them. Then, when they were through, she told them, repeating, as if fresh, a little sermon to abandon their search for help from humans. She told them to lament their condition as much as they needed and wanted, and leave it to Heaven to do now and later what it would. For no matter what we think, only the God of Abraham and Christ can turn stones into people.

Others came with conditions that only time could salve. There were those with hearts on fire. They wanted to kill someone—in their household or family, or a landlord or merchant who had cheated them. She soothed them; whatever season it was, she told them to wait a season, each of which, she said, held an advantage. In spring, life is a new stem. In the fall, the strongest trees bend but do not break in the winds.

Slowly but surely, her success won her an endearing nickname, Augurina—the little prophet. Her cures and advice and good will transformed suspicion into reliance. Her name spread through the region to smaller towns around.

Realizing her success could provoke jealousy among doctors, she was quick to refer patients to regional doctors. At the same time, she refused to offer opinions on land contracts, property disputes, arguments over wills, taxes, and village affairs. And fearing the powers of the local priest, she went out of her way to send those who had troubles with the church, God, any of the saints, or a remorseful conscience to him. Except those she took to be incurably ill, to whom she advised surrendering to the will of God, she let the priest offer advice about lighting candles, penance, and pilgrimages to Cefalù, Monreale, Palermo, and Mount Pellegrino with its Sanctuary of Santa Rosalia.

However, she threw caution to the wind when it came to advising individuals who asked her whether they should stay or leave Montemaggiore Belsito. On this matter she was near reckless with her advice. Most often she started with the firm directive, "Go! *Va via!*" And she continued, "In these mountains, in this village, things only stay the same. No one gets more land or more money, only work and scarcity. Everyone will get more poverty, disease, and misery." When they asked about emigrating to America, it was as if they plugged her into electricity; she lit up with energy. She commanded, "*Avanti! Avanti! Curaggio.* Conform your actions to your dreams," she counseled. "Here there are too many for too little! Here our children will spend their lives in the mountains and farming between the rocks. Only in folktales," Anna invariably added, "do small gardens grow miracles and magic beans grow ladders into heaven."

In advocating emigration, Augurina joined the side of a vast movement that swept the Madonie, all of Sicily, and southern Italy. The hour of departure was at hand. The people she told to go away wanted to go away. They were drawn by the tides of the sea below. In counseling emigration, Anna confirmed desires. As if christened by her passionate words, her clients left her patio with a spring in their step and a sparkle in their eyes. They would blurt out to the first person they encountered on the road, even when not asked,

"We will go. We will start a new life in America." Indeed, it was for this advice that Anna picked up the nickname Augurina and this name and her fame spread up and down the mountain slope as families of the ambitious poor rushed to start a better life in America. "*Augurina m'a dettu!*" was a phrase that increasingly resonated through the villages of the Madonie.

In the course of three years, Augurina's reputation grew. Her consultations went from one day to six days a week. Her life and her daughter's improved. She turned the small payments that often came to her in the form of bread, eggs, chickens, produce, and embroidered linen into money that she used as down payments on small connecting plots at the south end of town where she grew vegetables and artichokes and started a small olive orchard. In turn, she mortgaged these lands to borrow money to make additional down payments on other adjoining fields. When she added a second mule, cart, and two hired hands, she began regularly to transport emigrants and agricultural produce down the mountain to Palermo and occasional visitors and new goods up the mountain.

Aside from taking her daughter on holidays back and forth to the church school at Santa Rosalia in Cefalù, haulage became an integral part of her business. She delivered emigrants to port and delivered goods from Palermo and the nearer port of Termini Imerese. Saving the expense and chicanery of the middleman, she took her own crops directly to market and established and maintained stalls in Palermo's Vucc'iria market for her own crops. Special deliveries up and down the valley—which included everything from urgent love letters to a grand piano—also added money to her coffers. As a paved road, hand and hand with increased commerce, steadily advanced its way along the coast and toward the *bivio*, the crossroads, and the winding dirt and rock roads that led south and up the steady incline to Cerda, then small Aliminusa, and Montemaggiore Belsito, a dream awoke within her.

She would welcome the new traffic, which she believed would eventually come from below, with an inn and tavern that would stand at the northern entrance of Montemaggiore. Borrowing all the money she could, she flung herself into the project to make her dream come true. She consistently chose the best unwittingly as she planned her ten-room inn and the tavern, which more and more resembled a restaurant, with décor she bought in Palermo. Nothing equaled in extravagance the small crystal chandelier she purchased from an antiquities dealer.

For reasons buried in Palermo's bureaucracy, work stalled on the paved road and then came to a dead standstill. What had seemed at first a race along the coast abruptly halted and sunk in Sicily's ever-gathering oblivion. Augurina could not even find an official to discuss the plight of the road. Giving as good an explanation as any, Cucuzza declared, "The black serpent is too lazy to climb the mountain."

Augurina's creation was dead on the vine. Daily, she opened the door of her inn and tavern to no one. The locals stared at her building, as if a dead whale had washed up on the southern beach of town. Few ventured to eat at her place, and many of her clients stopped coming to seek her advice. They were at first amazed at and then resented the fact that their Augurina could have been so stupid and fail so miserably. Every time they saw the building they grew angry and ashamed, betrayed by their leader.

Failure awoke a pride that drove Augurina desperately to try to force the future. Captive of her own will, she committed herself to complete the inn and tavern. There was no one to tell her to stop, to turn her dream off. Even if someone had told her, it would have made no difference. She was determined to finish what she had started. The tavern and inn were ultimately not built of stone, wood, and glass. They were constructed out of her desire to regain her innocence, to get her revenge against this world, which had again betrayed her.

Like the losing gambler, her mounting debt drove her to gamble more and more. She was forced to sell off her land, then her mules and carts, and, finally, she recalled her daughter from school. What she had built in the course of ten years had come unraveled and turned to shambles in two. The word spread, "Augurina foretold everyone's fortune but her own." All enjoyed the story of the fortuneteller who misread her own fortune.

Disrespect for Augurina spread. Fewer and fewer relied on Augurina's services or advice. Up and down the valley, people spoke of "the auguress who couldn't augur." Cucuzza got it right when he joked she went from a shed to palace to hut. Augurina and her daughter were again disconnected from the town. They were reduced to tending their garden and chickens out back of the inherited shed and garden. The inn and tavern and everything else given over in mortgage had been confiscated by creditors.

Again a letter from Sebastianu and Paulina changed her fortune. She would send Angelina, now nineteen years old, to America. Althhough the letter contained two tickets, Anna sold one and gave the extra money from her ticket to Angelina. It didn't matter to Augurina that Angelina wanted to stay with her; she was inflexible: her daughter would leave this accursed land for America. And she promised, not quite believing what she said, that she would come later, soon, to join her.

When the day of departure arrived, Anna prepared Angelina for the cart that would take her to Palermo. After loading her trunk and case, she brought out from hiding the great crystal chandelier and loaded it, instructing Angelina, "Sell this in Palermo before you board the ship, pay the driver whatever you owe, and use what is left for a new life in America." As Angelina waved from the cart, which swayed and bumped its way around the first curve, the morning's light was caught and reflected back by the moving crystals of the chandelier. The refulgent sea waited below.

LA DESTINATA

Years passed and Angelina continued to live by spite.

During most of the year she hid her feelings from her fellow villagers, but as San Mauru's day drew near and Kelayres, the Pennsylvania coal town of 200, began to prepare for its annual August celebration, she could not disguise her spite.

Then she weeded the small garden of her Uncle Sebastianu and Aunt Paulina as if she intended to uproot the soil itself. When she went to shop, which she usually did on Tuesday morning, she would invariably insult the grocer, telling Malatesta that his bread was stale and his greens were spoiled. Malastesta knew enough not to dare to reply.

She chased the young children away from the front of her house with so many curses, calling them one and all, "*Figghi di Buttana!*" She displayed such vehemence that even the bravest of the children passed her house on the far side of the street.

Angelina even cursed the men of the village when their bocce game, which they played up and down the streets of Kelayres after supper during the summer, lingered too long in front of her place.

"*Baddi*"—her taunts were always about balls—"I am going to crush your little balls with a stick if you don't get out of here!" "Why don't you go home and let your wife roll your balls?"

Her profanity embarrassed the old men. They said that she was indecent. "*Manca rispittu. Porca sarvaggia!*" The young men would only smile slyly until they were free of the old men. Then they would laugh uproariously and talk about what they would like her to do to their balls. Pietro would always brag that she didn't have enough pasta for his saucy balls, but none of the boys believed him. The boys would end their discussion of her beauty with the chants of a fruit vendor: "Melons! Melons! / I have them red and sweet. / And to prove it, I'll slice them open. / Who really wants them tonight? / Slice them open!"

Everyone in village knew her story. Angelina was now thirty-four, yet still, in the villagers' words, as beautiful a woman as God had ever made—"*comu l'oru veru.*" Her fate had not altered her beauty. It had only added to it.

"At war with San Mauru." "*Guerra contra un santu*-whoever heard of such a thing?" the villagers asked.

They were angry at her for being at war with not just any saint, but their Saint, although only a few agreed on what miracles San Mauru performed. The old women believed that he helped you when you got the sweats, and at weddings they whispered among themselves about what a great lover he was until he fell in love with God. The younger people said he could stop your girlfriend from getting pregnant. Whenever a young man stood in prayer in front of the statue of San Mauru, gossip filled the village.

One villager believed San Mauru helped you find not only all you lost, but all you wanted to find. He swore that San Mauru regularly helped him find blueberries on the mountain. Also, he claimed San Mauru helped him find his wife, who—he insisted—had the best oven and bed in the whole village.

As much as villagers debated the powers of San Mauru, and even though some openly said San Mauru was not as powerful as he used to be—*menu forti ora*—no one, not even Tomasso the Doubter (*lu dubbiusu*), doubted San Mauru's ability still to do harm when angry. Yet there was not a single person, including the old, who didn't, at least at times, secretly sympathize with Angelina's fate. The entire village knew her story by heart.

18

For five years, from age nineteen when she was first brought to this country by her childless Uncle Sebastianu and Aunt Paulina, Angelina had done nothing but save money to bring her childhood sweetheart, Vincenzu, from Cerda, a mountain town in western Sicily, to her. She never spent a cent of the money she earned cleaning houses and cooking except for bedding for her trousseau and cloth for her wedding dress, which she and Paulina planned to sew together.

According to Sebastianu, she prayed four times a day to San Mauru that Vincenzu be able to come soon. She said special prayers before the statue of San Mauru after mass on Friday and Sunday. Father Ntoni was so impressed by her devotion that he gave her a small statue of San Mauru that she kept with her at all times.

Each year at the annual San Mauru's Day celebration, when the parish passed the statue through the streets of Kelayres, she rushed out and pinned money on San Mauru. Everyone knew her prayer: "San Mauru, bring me Vincenzu."

Seeing her once pin five dollars on the statue, her aunt Paulina taunted her for excess. "You have brought Vincenzu here already with the money you've put on San Mauru." Angelina simply replied, "San Mauru will reward me with Vincenzu."

Five years passed and finally the day arrived she had so long prayed for. She, along with Paulina and Sebastianu, made the trip to New York to get Vincenzu. On Ellis Island, they took their place in the great hall and, with hundreds of others, began their wait.

Four hours went by, and her wait turned into a vigil as the great hall emptied.

The longer she waited, the more she prayed. At first, she only glanced at the statue of San Mauru, who stuck out of the side of her purse. As the afternoon wore on, she clenched him in her hands, tearfully reminding him of her prayers and gifts. She implored him.

Each happy reunion around her seemed to move her a step closer to unhappiness. She prayed harder and harder that she be spared her terrible fear that there would be no Vincenzu.

Paulina and Sebastianu, in misery themselves, could do nothing to comfort her. "It was as if," Uncle Sebastianu remarked, "she were dead, *comu la morti,* as if her very spirit had gone out of her."

She woke from her trance only when her name echoed across the great empty hall, from the large megaphone suspended from the ceiling, "Angelina Ventimiglia! Or the party waiting for Vincenzu Baccialupu. Please come to Infirmary, Building Six."

The doctor explained: "We are sorry. There is nothing we can do—*nenti da fari.*"

"San Mauru, make it not true—*Non é viru!*" Angelina cried out, as she was to do many times in the following days.

The doctor took her to Vincenzu. This was not the Vincenzu who, the day before she left for America, passionately kissed her at the back of the orange orchard and told her that she was his life. In place of her fiery and fair Vincenzu lay a dying old man. Every breath he took seemed his last. His eyes were empty wells.

As the doctor predicted, Vincenzu died before morning. Uncle Sebastianu wired for money so they could bring Vincenzu's body back with them.

They arrived in Kelayres the following day. They sat three abreast in the front seat of the wagon. Vincenzu's wood casket lay in the back. It was as if they delivered death itself to the village.

Two days later, the whole village buried Vincenzu in the small Italian cemetery at the foot of the mountain. People ate the traditional meal prepared by Sebastianu and Paulina's cousins. The only audible sounds, other than the steady hush of whispering that came from the old women huddled together in commiseration, was Angelina's bitter lamentation.

She cried and cried, until her grief turned to hate. "Pain watered her hate," Paulina added.

Angelina became more beautiful in her grief. Her blue eyes became bluer, her black hair blacker. She became "*Mafiusa!*" the men commented. "The fiery furnace of sorrow has made her as beautiful and hard as a diamond!" Turiddu Dentilupu, the town poet, remarked.

It was during this period of her metamorphosis that the villagers started to call Angelina *La Destinata*, the fated one. God had singled her out. She was a jewel shining anger.

Angelina continued to work as much as before, for she had to repay Uncle Sebastianu for the expense of bringing back and burying Vincenzu.

La Destinata spent her evenings on the porch and in the garden. She never smiled. She quit going to church. She would never say more than a few words to Father Ntoni, no matter what effort he made to engage her in conversation.

On San Mauru's Day, La Destinata would take up her post on the porch early and look daggers at everyone passing by on the way to church. Under her breath, she cursed them for worshipping the saint who had betrayed her.

Later, when the parish procession passed, her hate truly radiated for all to see. "She pins curses on the Saint with her glances," said Tomasso. Pregnant women were afraid to get anywhere between San Mauru and La Destinata's glance. Even some of the parish's boldest men were afraid to assume the honorary position of carrying San Mauru for fear of crossing her glance.

Her hate was so palpably intense that the heads of the San Mauru Society kept the saint under lock and key during the days immediately preceding his festival. The people of Kelayres feared for their saint. They worked themselves up telling stories of believers who had attacked saints. Sam Salamanga, who had more tales than anyone in Kelayres, told how one fisherman in the Golfu de Castellamare covered the statue of Saint Rosalia with fish tails when his fishing boat sank.

To the village's astonishment, exactly ten years after the death of Vincenzu, Angelina went to mass one Sunday. She sat on the right side of the church, directly in front of San Mauru. It appeared that she prayed to him. She did the same thing the following Sunday and the Sunday after. Rumors spread throughout town. "La Destinata is reconciled with San Mauru."

The young men concluded, "La Destinata is again ready for a man." And each pretended that he could be that man. "*É na lupina amabili*—a wolf to love," Sariddu said especially loudly to disguise the fear mounting within him as he thought about being alone with La Destinata.

"If she is reconciled, why doesn't she ever take communion?" the clever Giuvanni Vecchione, the head of the Sons of Italy club, asked. No one ever had an answer for his question. So his question became the signal to start their evening game of bocce.

The village spent much of its free time debating what would happen next until one Tuesday evening in October. At the club, in the presence of Sebastianu, Giuvanni revealed what Father Ntoni had confided to him that morning:

"The preceding Saturday afternoon, just as he was leaving the confessional, Father Ntoni saw Angelina approach San Mauru, reverently pin twenty to his breast, and then mock, taunt, and curse him as no saint has ever been cursed.

"'You have no power to do anything. You are saint nobody, *Santu Nuddu*! You are just a chunk of plaster. Your eyes, ears, mouth, and prick are dead. *Mortu. Mortu.* I give you this money. I stand

22

right before you and insult you to your face, and you do nothing. *Santu Nuddu!* You are an impotent do-nothing ball-less, saint.'

"Then she spat in the face of San Mauru and left."

Upon hearing this, Sebastianu stumbled and almost fell over. He was short of breath. He could barely walk the short distance home.

"Spitting at our Saint, Angelina!" Sebastianu shouted as he entered the backdoor. And then he pleaded with her, "In the name of all we have done for you, don't spit on San Mauru. Please apologize to him."

"Apologize to him, or curse him? It doesn't matter. He is nothing but a plaster *imputenti*," La Destinata replied. "I am already thirty-four, and I am without man or child because of him."

Not knowing what to reply, Sebastianu put on his cap and went out to hoe his garden, which he always did when he was distressed.

Paulina stayed in the corner of the living room and nervously prayed the rosary. The beads were her garden. And silence ruled the house.

Three weeks later, on a Sunday afternoon, the priest appeared at Sebastianu and Paulina's door. They feared the worst as they saw him mount the stairs with a man in his early forties. At first glance they thought perhaps the stranger was a representative of San Mauru or some other high official. Like a peasant dressed in his best, the strange man wore a dark blue suit that was hardly able to contain his large shoulders and big arms. He wore bright, shiny black shoes, which were worn only for weddings, funerals, and other important occasions.

Wasting no time, Father Ntoni quickly explained. Felici, Felici Benfattu, here, is from Hazelton, San Mauru's parish. He has a steady job, in the grocery warehouse. Anyhow, he lost his wife last month. She died giving birth to their first son. Now he is alone with four young children. He needs a wife who is smart, who can cook, clean, and be a good woman. His parish priest asked if I could help him find such a wife. So that is why we are here.

Neither Sebastianu nor Paulina could quite believe what they heard. A joke, a trap, a dream? Surely it seemed too good to be true! Not knowing what to believe or what to say, dumbfounded, they simply looked back and forth at each other until the priest said: "*Allura*, well, is Angelina here?"

"Get Angelina," Sebastianu shouted to Paulina. And then, as if she had not just heard it herself, he said, "Tell her the priest is here with a"—Sebastianu hesitated—"*un omu onuratu di* San Mauru, in Hazelton."

Several minutes passed and Paulina did not reappear with Angelina. Sebastianu grew fearful. Perhaps Angelina would throw a fit—get mad, curse, and not come out. At least, thank goodness, he heard no shouting, and there was creaking in her room above.

Finally, after what seemed an hour to Sebastianu, Paulina led Angelina into the living room. Her head was down and she was wearing her best dress. The visitor, who stood partially behind the large priest, looked down as well.

Sebastianu trembled to think what would happen when they looked up. Felici raised his eyes first. Then, a second later, Angelina raised hers. When their eyes met there was no doubt for Sebastianu, Paulina, or Father Ntoni what had occurred. It was there to be seen in the meeting of their eyes.

As the priest introduced them and Sebastianu poured glasses of his homemade wine, Paulina thought of what kind of wedding dress she could sew from the cloth stored in Angelina's trousseau.

Their courtship was shortened to a month—just enough time to get the three required church vows read. "Meant for each other—*Dio la voli*, God wants it," everyone said. "As certain as the stars and moon and sun are in the sky," Turiddu Dentilupu said, and added, making sure everyone heard his bit of cleverness, "*Destinata é Destinata.*"

A month later, before a full church, Angelina and Felici stood before the priest. The three of them stood below San Mauru. Never before had a marriage occurred there, but Angelina had insisted.

As the priest read the prayers, Angelina continually smiled and kept looking back and forth at Felici and San Mauru. Observing the visible sign of her equal affection for Felici and San Mauru, the parishoners' eyes filled with tears. Even Giuseppina Messina cried. Long after the wedding, Carmella Notaro continued to claim that she had seen a tear in San Mauru's right eye. Sam Salamagna alone dissented, "I never heard of a saint who cried out of only one eye. You must have missed seeing the tears in his other eye."

As Angelina and Felici left the church, the witnesses to the blessed event first softly whispered and then chanted loudly, "*Miraculu! Miraculu!*"

On the stairs of the church, the children and women threw rice at the new couple. Off to one side, the young men, softly but with a quickening rhythm, rehearsed the fruit peddler's chant. "There go the best melons in town—*russie, duci*, red and sweet."

Hearing them, Angelina winked and smiled, as she stepped up into the horsedrawn carriage, which by the day's end would take her from Kelayres to Hazelton and her new life. Felici, her husband, sat next to her like a prince, while his youngest daughter played with the sequins on Angelina's dress.

As the carriage left, Paulina and Sebastianu cried and the villagers shouted, "Long live San Mauru." Angelina turned, looked back, and waved again. In her hand was her small statue of San Mauru.

FLIGHT INTO THE ELEMENTS

"Run! Run!" they hollered. How long, how far, and to where, Vincenzu wasn't sure, but he ran and ran. By nightfall, he found himself near Termini Immeresi. That night he slept out in a field of tall grass and ruins where, twenty-five hundred years before, Siracusans had slaughtered Carthaginians.

Chilled, shivering, he awoke under a canopy of stars whose still and distinct beams contrasted with his agitated mind. His compass of possibilities warned only that he couldn't go home. The police presumed in their dealings with country folk that everyone returns home, if not within a week, then in the coming fall when all hands are called to the harvest. Every village also has an informer, Vincenzu thought.

Vincenzu couldn't put out of his fear-driven mind two contradicting and oscillating thoughts: how much his mother, sister, and brother could use him and, of great weight, how far his flight—perhaps to forever—was carrying him from his betrothed Angelina and from America, which his very nickname, *Vadu a l'America*, pledged him. Yet come the first light of morning, he would run. Reasons offered no brakes against the momentum of fear.

Vincenzu followed the coast into the rising sun as best he could, avoiding settlements and main roads. In the afternoon the great rock promontory and the town of Cefalù, which he knew meant "the rock," loomed ahead. Vincenzu recognized his impending choice: he must move upland into the lower mountains to circle the town or actually enter the town and find shelter.

Exhausted and hungry and uncertain, step by step Vincenzu slowed down. Dizzy, he almost toppled onto a patch of sand, coffin size, cast between the shallow beds of eroded limestone crisscrossing the beach between curved walls of rock that formed one small bay after another. As he rested, deposited stones protruded into his body, while the slap and suck of crashing waves stole his rest and pulled his Angelina away into the deep underside of the sea.

At the zigzag border of being half awake and asleep, a single thought buoyed up in his mind. A hope, a possibility, a moment's life raft: just perhaps his old friend and mentor Father Malatesta—or as he was known by the children of Cerda, Falcone, the priest with a great beak of a nose—was still teaching in Cefalù.

Vincenzu worked his way from the beach to the narrow black stone streets, past the Fisherman's Port, to the cathedral, next to which stood the seminary. He timidly knocked at its great door. One moment he was knocking at the door; the next, he was staring directly into the nose of Falcone. As if the distance of five years didn't count or the possibility of someone overhearing didn't matter, Vadu a l'America blurted out the story of his flight.

With his chin resting on the knuckles of his hands, which were perched on top of his amply-knotted staff of wild pear, Vincenzu told his story. He told how with single swats he killed the two men in the Palermo market who not only refused to pay his brother and him but pulled knives on them when he tried to collect for the family's artichokes.

Almost without hesitating, he went on to tell of his romance with Angelina and his promise to join her as soon as he could in Pennsylvania. Falcone did not condemn Vicenzu's deed, his flight from the untrustworthy law, and he would not deny such an earnest young man's first love. With a long sigh, the priest issued one great and slightly humorous "alas," alluding to all his efforts to lure Vincenzu into the priesthood: "We are never to have you, Vadu a l'America, as a priest."

With a cautious temperament that fostered prudence, Falcone did not welcome outlaw Vincenzu into the seminary. But he proposed that Vincenzu stay in one of several huts up behind the cathedral, where a handful of homeless individuals roosted for years or just single nights. The cathedral supplied food and occasional repairs to the primitive dwellings out of the poor box.

So Vincenzu began his life under the shadow of the rock. In the morning he went to the shore to wash and reflect on the sea that blocked and permitted his crossing to Angelina. He thought how deep, cruel, and indifferent the sea whose waves mechanically cracked on the reaching shore and then sloshed and sucked their churning way through the irregular beds of eroded rock.

The beach for him was unbearably bright. It would not grant anything a shadow. Worse, water for Vincenzu was a great hypocrite. It wore all faces, made all promises. It offered itself as a great giving font—ever ready to bathe, refresh, and renew; and yet it was treacherous, ever ready to drag you out, pull you down, drown you, and feed you to the crabs and fast-running pipers. It stole all certitude from the world. Christ walked on the stormy sea, while other mortals, like the apostles, feared drowning.

After washing at the beach Vincenzu would go to mass. He would constantly look up at the mosaic of the Pantocrator. But no matter how he read the Pantocrator's eyes, Vincenzu did not see the slightest trace of mercy or promise of miracle.

On Sundays Vincenzu climbed the great rock. It took energy to climb, especially when it was cold and wet. Then he would wheeze, and at points the path was treacherously slippery. A sharp and stiff wind often crowned his ascent. The view from on high did not console him. Rather, it reminded him how far he was from home and

Angelina. With each visit to the rock, Vincenzu only grew in certainty that the rock was hard, proud, and indomitable—enemy of all that was soft.

On one of his Sunday descents from the great rock of Cefalù, at the upper edge of town Vincenzu was greeted by an approaching priest: "Are you Vincenzu, friend of Father Malatesta?" No sooner had Vincenzu replied, "*Si, patri miu*," than the priest took a grip on his arm and said, "Father Malatesta says that you are strong, tenacious, and intelligent. Is that true? Do you have keen eyes for the difference of things?"

Vincenzu took a deep breath and replied, "I am very strong. I have always worked and hoed the land. I pray that I can believe and think straight. And," Vincenzu rushed to add, "I see the forms that God's light of day puts before me."

"Good! You can come with me, Vincenzu. I will feed and house you as we travel the Madonie, searching and collecting minerals and fossils. At the end of four months, at the beginning of June, I will give you $75—$25 dollars now, $25 halfway through our work, $25 at shipside in Palermo, where I will put you on a ship disguised as an illiterate mountaineer bound for America." Without hesitation the rapid-speaking priest said in one breadth, "*D'accordo? Andiamo!*"

Nodding and saying yes, Vincenzu had no idea with whom he had just contracted a deal. He only knew for sure that he had been promised a miracle—to get to America and his Angelina—and that he had contracted with *Testa in Giù*, Head-Down, the priest who looked for rocks everywhere.

As they went together to assemble their gear and supplies for their forthcoming trip to the Madonie, the priest's nickname stood forth. With his head down, which had won him the nickname *Testa in Giù*, he scanned the white lines and semi-circles for fossils in the black marble that paved the main road. He treated the cathedral

29

stairs themselves not as the front door to God's kingdom but as the entrance into the depths of the ocean's rock, which existed before the Mediterranean. Once inside the cathedral, the priest sought a fossil treasury of the Jurassic. He rubbed his hands up and down the red columns looking for specimens. Almost in ecstasy the priest examined the cathedral's great ancient red baptismal font as a treasury of ammonites.

He exclaimed far beyond the comprehension of Vincenzu, "We baptize our babies in iron-red two-hundred-million-year Jurassic seas!" in which ammonites thrived in the protection of their chambered homes while ancient sharp *squali* with teeth-filled mouths the size of a man prowled the sea.

As Vincenzu passed days with the priest, assembling their provisions, he grew accustomed to the priest's ground-surveying periscope glance, abrupt stops, and constant declarations and proclamations. He constantly blurted out fragments of sentences as he bore witness to epiphanies and announced revelations about rocks and fossils. No doubt his mind belonged to the wonders of geology.

Vincenzu and the priest set out on the steep path for Isnello. His road went due south to Sant di Gibilmanna, under the shadow of Peak San Angelo, which soared to more than 3000 feet to Isnello which, at more than 1600 feet, was the throat of the mountain that crowned the valley that sloped down to Cefalù and its coasts.

In the evenings Testa in Giù, lubricated by his third glass of local wine, lectured Vincenzu on geology. Rocks, he told Vincenzu, who filled, carried, and loaded the large rough canvas bags of his specimens, can all be distinguished by traits of color and hardness and their crystals and composition. In his more pedagogic moments he didactically explained that there were sedimentary rocks; exemplified by sandstone and limestone, they formed accumulated layers, compressed beds that were found in beaches and bays and off shore and deep in the sea, created from the skeletons of coral, shells, and other marine life.

On select occasions, the slightly inebriated priest treating rock-hauling Vincenzu as colleague, he elaborated on metamorphic rocks formed deep below under great weight and pressure and the melting and flow of crystallizing minerals. He repetitiously returned to speak of red rocks, which were identified with iron-stained Jurassic seas. Light-headed with wine around the embers of an evening fire in the cooling oak groves above Isnello, he waxed on to speak of the magic of two hundred million years ago and the birth of Sicily. As if to stun the world with a secret of the ages, Testa in Giù shouted over the crackling and sparking campfire that some geologists say that these very mountains still have the fossils of elephants, rhinoceros, and crocodiles proving that Sicily's mother was the continent Africa. And with a fourth glass of wine, Testa in Giù, as if reduced to re-peating snake stories, repeated that in blood-red Jurassic seas there were ammonites secure in compartmentalized chambers and free-roaming giant big-toothed sharks—*megalodons,* fifty feet long—that swam and ruled the sea.

As Testa in Giù daily followed his love of rocks, so Vicenzu, in-wardly and subconsciously, grew to hate rocks. For Vincenzu rocks were by origin and end a single dark and opposing element, a god bent on warring against woman, earth—all that was kind, soft, tender, worthy of embracing. It was as if Etna, clandestine and eruptive, had captured his dreams: rocks spewed forth with flying firebombs, scalding rivers of molten lava, and clouds of ash that blackened the sun.

Rock, in his dreams, would never relent. It ruled adamantly be-low, sovereign and hegemonic in its hidden and clandestine ways. Rock would crush man, valley, earth, and even fill the seas.

Vincenzu saw himself, as Sicilian peasants and shepherds commonly do, as being permanently at war against rock. Fields and garden forever must be cleared of stone and rock. The points of ploughs break and dull on rock; hopes of winning slivers of soil are desperately worked for. Shepherds and their animals must forever climb the rock and scratch their lives out of the grass between it. You must build your house out of the same cold hard rock.

Vincenzu could not think of his life past or present separate from a personal war against rock: rock stood in the way of his obligations to his fatherless family—to aid his brother in securing ownership of the land and provide a dowry for his two sisters. Rock stood in the way now of reaching the soft valley of Angelina and the open and fertile ground of America.

As his vision of spreading rock metastasized, he began to dream of the soft, fleshy breasts and thighs of Angelina petrifying. He envisioned sheets of bedrock bursting forth in the flattening, widening, desirable valley that lay just below his own Cerda. Rock, Vincenzu blurted out, was the real cross of life. All the saints, and Mary, Saint Peter, the rock himself, and Jesus cannot free man from bursts of rising outcroppings and avalanches.

On the southeastern reaches of Isnello, where man sculpted stone into Santa Maria Maggiore and a castle lies at the base of six hundred feet of sheer rock, Vincenzu began to cough and lightly rasp. Even when awake he grew claustrophobic about the towering rocks that surrounded him.

Staying one night at the nearby Grotta Abbisso del Vento, Vincenzu fantasized about the brown bats that covered sections of its walls and high ceiling in patches. Always afraid of bats, he branded them with the metaphor birds of darkness. And extending this notion, he took their exits from the cave as helter-skelter demonic missions from interior and chaotic depths of rock against the world of light and soaring flight. Horrid dreams followed these fantasies. In one dream, he dropped a stone down a hole in the cavern floor. Here was a true well of darkness. It had no bottom. There light vanished—captured souls turned to cold stone, and lovers divided forever. In another dream, which he had more than once, he kept losing his sheep. One of the sheep entrusted to him was stalked by a "wolf-bear" that abruptly turned on Angelina, ripping out her filthy black and green wool intestines on which tomatoes grew. He awoke coughing and screaming: "*Zi, zi, aviti luci?*" (Uncle, uncle, do you have light?) "*Di, Di, aviti luci?*" (God, God, do you have light?)

One night at the campfire Vincenzu's turbulent mind burst forth in words. Uninvited, unannounced, he started out:

"We live on and in rock. Look at the altars of the church. Even Cefalù's Christ Panocrator, the great Lord, is assembled in small stones. The only thing men on this island know is to entomb themselves in rock, stone, brick, tile, cement. They form the walls that enclose their gardens, homes, and churches and make the roofs and floors of buildings. And fieldstone and rock dredged from the sea make our roads.

"We, the poor, know this, for we forever work and bruise ourselves on rock. It is our hurt and futility. Everywhere stone sounds and echoes lives.

"We strip the lands of woods to cut and frame stone—and," he hesitated, beginning to break off his speech, "to build the ships to carry us from this rock-infested land to a world rich in soft valleys and my Angelina."

The priest listened silently as Vincenzu finished and began to cough and cry. Testa in Giù knew, even though a week before their planned return to Cefalù, the hour had come to take Vincenzu down out of the mountains and send him to America.

As they began their long and slow descent, which would lead first to Cefalù, where they would drop off cartloads of the priest's specimens before continuing on to the docks of Palermo, Vincenzu began to cough more and more. His coughing spells grew worse as they left Cefalù.

Palermo almost blinded now-feverish Vincenzu with a riot of scenes, sounds, and colors. It forced him, dizzy and delirious, to hold more tightly to the carriage the priest had borrowed from the seminary.

With the priest acting as a spokesman for Vincenzu, he started by saying Vincenzu spoke limited Italian. The agent, deferential to the priest, automatically wrote down Vincenzu's falsified name and village, and wrote down answers given to his one-word questions. Occupation? "*Pastore.*" Literate? "Barely, he can read a few words." Destination? "He is going to Pennsylvania to join his cousins in the coal mines." "*Augurin e buon viaggio!*" the agent said, stamping Vincenzu's documents. He could not resist taunting Vincenzu a little, "Do you intend to be a shepherd in America?" "Why?" puzzled Vincenzu. "Everyone doesn't take a wild pear walking stick, *una bastone de pera selvatica,* to America." "These clodhoppers! (*questi rustici!*)," whispered the agent to a fellow agent. "God bless America, and the Columbus who discovered it."

Vincenzu had not coughed or wheezed once during the brief interrogation. Testa in Giù gave Vincenzu a hug and slipped a lucky crystal in his pocket. No sooner had Vincenzu climbed the wood gangplank than he was assigned a bunk number below and told that he should store his stick under his bed. The ship, he was instructed, would sail at 8:00 the next morning, *appunto.*

Vincenzu descended the narrow metal stairs and followed the tight aisle to his place: the bottom bed, in the last bunk, at the end of the far row. He need only stand to look out a small port window, but he was a long way from the toilet. Tiredness nagged at him. He put his stick and cloth sack under his bunk, unrolled his two blankets, and put on warm clothes to protect himself against the dank, clanging cave of steel. Exhausted from the journey, Vincenzu fell fast asleep and woke only with the shuddering of the steamship getting underway.

The breeze from land was stiff, the sky spelled rain, and Vincenzu dreaded the blue landless horizon that lay ahead. He feared telling anyone, including the ship's doctor, about his illness; and there was no refuge on deck or below. Below, foul smells magnified, the noise of crying children went uninterrupted, and all the time his weakness increased and his shivering and sweating intensified. The hull was sepulcher worse than the rocky Grotta Abbisso del Vento. There was no forest to retreat to. Above, he found himself on the surface of a rolling ship, its roll and pitch made severe by fall seas. His mind moved between its empty horizons and unfathomable depths, deeper than the origins of rocks. Press his mind as strongly as he could, he could not imagine Angelina before him, not even for an instant, or hold onto the simplest prayers. Lapping waves and escalating fevers stole his mind, which increasingly told him that even the sight of rock would be a comfort.

So days and nights, wakening and dreams, mingled and jumbled. Vincenzu spent more and more time in his bunk. He had less and less a clear idea that he was on a ship and sailing the sea. More and more, he only wanted the shivers, sweats, and bouts of coughing and wheezing to end. At some point, he was transferred to sickbay, where kind hands administered medicines and mumbled foreign words. He awoke the last time to shouting filling the cavernous dormitory of the hull: Land ahoy! America ahead! And then there was a glimpse and the whispered smell of his soft and comforting Angelina.

WAR OF THE SAINTS

The young priest Antonino Benfattu received his first assign-
ment at Immaculate Conception in Kelayres. This was the very par-
ish of his immigrant Ziu Sebastianu and Zia Paulina, who had wel-
comed his mother, Angelina, to America as a young woman. It was
also a homeground for San Mauru, the saint in whom Angelina had
placed such trust since her arrival in 1893 to deliver her betrothed,
Vincenzu. San Mauru was also the saint she publicly despised when,
after five years of praying to him and waiting for Vincenzu, her be-
trothed was delivered dead—dead within the very day of arrival at
Ellis Island and his transfer to the island's hospital. And then again
she was grateful and devoted to San Mauru for his gift of her hus-
band, Felici Benfattu, and her life in Hazelton and its San Mauru's
parish there.

Antonino was reporting to San Mauru's fresh from a month's
tour of Sicily. After a year studying at a Vatican institute for theology
in Rome, he traveled to Sicily, where he first visited the estate of his
great-grandfather Don Dottore Antonio Ventimiglia of Valle dell'
Olmo, who had died unreconciled with his daughter. From his
great-grandfather's abandoned and uncared-for estate, well on its
way to joining Sicily's abundant Baroque ruins, which flourished
when Spain ruled, Antonino traveled over the southern Madonie
mountains to Montemaggiore to visit the small garden of Sebastianu
and Paulina, where his grandmother had first found refuge and
made her own fortune as a renowned regional healer and fortune
teller, until she squandered all she had made and saved on a hotel
and restaurant meant to capture travelers along a road never built.

Antonino took to Sicily as if he belonged there, even though he assembled his speech from phrases he had heard as boy, grammatical Italian learned hastily in Rome, and guesses based on Latin. Nevertheless, the animated gestures reminded him of family, and the elemental contrasts between sky and land, rock and greens, grapevines and olive trees, pines and palms filled him with energy. Everything vividly etched itself on his brain, as if it already belonged to his deepest memory.

Once the villagers were assured that he had not returned to lay claim to his late grandmother's restaurant and small hotel, which they had transformed into a community clubhouse, they treated him as a favorite son. They toured him around the town and countryside, home by home and garden and field by garden and field. They fed him endless meals based on greens, beans, *caponata*, and artichokes.

They organized a great farewell feast for him at the club after the celebration of a special mass by the local priest, Paffu Zoppu, who was quite fat, had a terrible limp, and more than once in the past few years had fallen down the altar steps, during communion. Then, after a concert of five trumpets, two baritones, three trombones, and a drum (all the local musicians Montemaggiore could summon), they held a dance. Antonino danced with all the women, young and old. Scruples about pleasure roiled up his mind, but they did not stop his dizzying whirling feet or suppress the pleasure of bumping up against a soft breast, holding a fresh hand, and catching the sparkle of a flirting eye. While he danced with more gusto than providence, surely entering onto the territory of venial sin, he enjoyed himself thoroughly.

Children dodged in and out of the crowd, eating the sweets they could get their greedy hands on. With the exception of a few "city slickers" who had their hair pasted back and danced with the clever glides and presumptuous postures of Palermo dance halls, most men conducted their dancing partners onto the floor as if they were bridled donkeys and mules, and heavily stepped around the floor indifferent to their partner's constant coaxing. Old men, freed from the duty of dancing, leaned back in chairs and, warmed by more than a healthy quota of wine, heatedly discussed the promise of this year's olive, fig, and wine harvest, *la vendemmia*. They also by convention made jokes about their halcyon days when they hunted in the distant mountain forest and chased young women in nearby valleys.

Toothless old women, who had put on their second and best black shawls, huddled at the back of the room like a party of grackles. They erratically emitted raw and hoarse laughs, which all knew arose from their titillating speculations about how well the young priest would do in bed if he were unfettered by church and collar. He might be as good as a well-endowed sailor or the strong blacksmith who heated the forge and pounded the anvil. Prompted by such merrymaking, one older woman speculated aloud for all to hear: "He dances too well to keep his cassock on forever!"

The festival concluded with toasts to Father Antonino; his grandmother, Augurina; his mother, Angelina; and America—and Pennsylvania and Kelayres, wherever they were, too! The local priest issued the common customary blessing for a long trip, so frequently given up and down the mountain before the war in the great period of emigration. The mayor, who wore a coat, a sort of admiral's hat, and a sword for the occasion, gave a practiced "come-again farewell" speech. The evening, which concluded without even mention of the world depression or Mussolini, was informally ended by Old Toto spontaneously shouting out, having had five glasses of wine: "One of ours goes far but never leaves the hearth of our heart." And, as everyone cheered, he added under his breath: "But some of you bastards would trade your own mother for a jug of olive oil. Myself, I would need a gallon of wine."

At last Father Antonino was heading down the slope to Cerda and then Palermo to return by steamship to America—to Kelayres, Pennsylvania, where lived the Amatos, the Rizzutos, the Pernas, the Brucatos, the Notaros, so many other families from the mountain villages of the Madonie and adjacent regions.

At age twenty-four he was ready to begin his ministry. He would leave the safe and secluded kingdom of the church and the realm of words and theology for a life in the village among the people. He would now depart from the level road of the seminary to follow the sinuous path of people's everyday lives and hearts. He embraced the idea that hereafter his real home would only be his trust in God. He cherished the notion that he would care for hearts as his grandmother and great grandfather had cared for bodies.

Antonino arrived in a parish that had turned into a battleground. As the Sicilians, the traditional supporters of San Mauru at Immaculate Conception, left for Buffalo, Rochester, and Detroit, the more recently arrived Neapolitans, who stayed in Kelayres, increasingly affirmed the importance of San Gennaro. Starting with a small painting and candleholder along the back wall of the church dedicated to their patron saint Gennaro, they had, at their own expense, succeeded in advancing his cause. They bought a larger and better painting of their patron saint and replaced the five-flat candelabra with an inclined ten-row candelabra, which held not only the traditional small ten-cent candles but also supported an upper row of the giant one-dollar candles, which, when the drafts in the church diminished, burned for as long as two weeks. And just as Father Antonino arrived the rivalry between the supporters of San Mauru and upstart San Gennaro was really heating up, as the newcomers let it be known that they had just ordered a four-hundred-dollar life-size statue of their patron saint from Naples. It was their intention to place him at the front of the church in the alcove on the left. This would not only displace the Sicilians' favorite Saint Joseph—and land him in the dingy basement!—but it would put San Gennaro on the same footing as San Mauru, who stood in the front alcove on the right.

The war of saints spread quickly and deeply in the community and soon reached the schoolyard, where every lunch recess witnessed two opposing groups of children standing at different ends of the baseball diamond, along first and third base, hurling taunts at one another until the teacher called them in. In all fairness, it must be confessed that the Neapolitan children were the principal aggressors. Spurred on by their parents' mounting offense to place San Gennaro on equal footing in the church and alongside the altar with San Mauru, they felt they too must do their share. Feeling they enjoyed the superior hand in this war of words, they initiated the daily and ritualized conflict by challenging the Sicilian adherents of San Mauru to name significant miracles he had accomplished. Caught like most defenders of tradition in a situation in which their best argument was best if left unvoiced, they lacked crisp ideas to raise on behalf of their cause. Their puny listing that San Mauru cures gout, helps the deaf, allows miners to see in the dark, helps with constipation—and, in fact, he recently allowed Antonella Facella to find her husband in the night at the bottom of a deep ditch where he lay drunk and in danger of drowning in the waters of the rising ditch—only increased the chiding of their opponents. They punctuated each claim on behalf of San Mauru's prowess and deeds with a predictable "That's nothing!" (*"C'e nenti, c'e nenti!"*) And they greeted the claim that San Mauru once cured Filippo DiBlasi's horse, which had recently died en route from Kelayres to Hazelton, of the heaves, with "That's a double nothing. The only thing that lazy horse, *cavullu pigru*, did was eat oats and fart."

The youthful enthusiasts for San Gennaro, who was, as even the ignorant followers of San Mauru should know, Naples' most famous saint, reveled in their chance to proclaim their patron. San Gennaro, no common recent saint, was a real Roman martyr. When the wild beasts in the arena wouldn't eat him, the Romans beheaded him. To this day, his blood kept in a vial in Naples' cathedral liquefies eighteen times a year. And when it does liquefy it foretells another good year for all of Naples and its grape harvest, and more than once it has stopped the eruption of Mount Vesuvius in its tracks. And Vesuvius puts Sicily's Etna to shame, they added. It did this, they elaborated with glee, by its size, discharge, and the sheer destruction it wrought through the years.

Some Sicilian old-timers voiced resignation about the coming of San Gennaro. With a deeply rehearsed fatalism, they said God will let happen what happens, dressing the idea up with an old proverb: *Lu Celu mi jttau, et la terra m'apparu*—Heaven seeded me and the earth harvested me. Contradicting the old fatalists, younger Sicilians argued that these pessimistic exaggerators, who had learned to prosper by the work of their own hands—and once couldn't afford soap or toilet paper, and, to use one of their favorite and freshly learned English expressions, didn't have a pot to piss in—now surrendered with their hands held high to the sky. Anyhow, the old replied that the ship bringing San Gennaro would probably sink en route. Furthermore, they reasoned, if San Mauru has the power we think he has, he won't allow it. He will smash San Gennaro to smithereens. We will light a candle or two to see that he does exactly that. Pietro Brucato, whose dark complexion, recessed eyes, and slow manner of speaking matched his philosophical temperament, sounded his own trumpet when he declared, "Two people, two saints, and we still all light candles, although not everyone pays for the candles they pray for." No one knew exactly what this meant, therefore it was unimpeachable and a matter of whole-hearted assent and enthusiastic agreement.

The majority of the supporters of San Mauru did not embrace resignation. The mere mention of the coming of San Gennaro ignited their anger. When they heard the Neapolitans sing the praises of San Gennaro, especially his power to cure impotence, or worse, score San Mauru for failing to stave off the bad economic times that had fallen on them and the world, their blood boiled. Conversations about the saint from Naples—a town of sailors, whores, and sinners—stoked inner fires and further deepened the split between the Sicilian and the Neapolitan members of the Sons of Italy. The bocce games out back all seemed like grudge matches, the way the heavy wooden balls were thrown and collided so harshly.

In fact, the day Father Antonino arrived in Kelayres was the very day the Neapolitan parishioners returned from New York with the statue of San Gennaro. The Sicilian parishioners mistook the jubilant beeping and shouting announcing the arrival of the San Gennaro as the greeting they expected would welcome Father Antonino. They suffered a double disappointment when, arriving at the church, they found not only no new priest but instead had to stand by the curb and watch the Neapolitans joyously and boisterously remove San Gennaro from his large crating case. Then, as if to add insult to injury, they ever so slowly unpacked him only to solemnly lift him onto a wheeled and decorated platform, which they had secretly built and painted in a nearby garage.

The followers of San Gennaro hastily assembled a band and announced, no doubt following their long-laid hidden plans, the spontaneous beginning of an initiation parade for San Gennaro. Good-natured Sicilian-born accordion player Paul De Carlo doubled the outrage to his own kind when, turncoat that he was, he led the band all around town—on the very same route San Mauru had followed since he was first installed in Immaculate Conception forty years before. To further infuriate the Sicilians, the Neapolitans, who were judged always to be crying poor mouth when it came to support of the church, pinned oodles of money on San Gennaro. They also knelt at the side of the road with a fervor they never displayed before when San Mauru came by or even when they took communion on Easter.

By the time Father Antonino arrived, as the parade was concluding in front of the church, a full squabble was occurring on the church steps. The Sicilians, having taken up a place on the front church steps, had formed a wall blocking the admission of the statue into the church, and the principal advocates of San Gennaro tried to push their way forward. Adding to the commotion, Bocciacalup, lifting a sledge hammer over his head, threatened to smash San Gennaro to smithereens if they took one step forward. Truly, things had reached an angry impasse, just as Father Antonino showed up.

Greeted by a cacophony of shouts and imprecations of every sort and skyward gestures accompanying pledges and curses, the new priest found the wit to encourage all to sit down and choose a representative from each camp to make its case. After considerable argument over who should go first, a proponent for San Gennaro began. He detailed all the good the saint had done in the old country for fertility and the birth of healthy babies and promised the same for all the parishioners of Immaculate Conception. The advocate of San Mauru, not wishing to risk the wrath of San Mauru or San Gennaro, told how a church in Sicily ended up with two of everything—two women's sodalities, rosary societies, and twin recreation centers—and eventually two separate churches, which both exceeded the means of their parishioners. Then, getting to the heart of his argument, he asked whether San Gennaro would have a parade of his own and who would control the money pinned on him.

Father Antonino recognized how problematic this all could become. He suggested that they put both San Gennaro, who was to be introduced, and Saint Joseph, who was to be demoted to the rear of the church, in the basement, back to back, until a decision could be reached. One of San Gennaro's advocates argued, "Not in the coal bin!" and another couldn't resist shouting out from the anonymity of the crowd, "In the very same basement your mother attacked San Mauru?" Others wondered aloud how a Sicilian priest, whose mother was a devotee to San Mauru, could render a fair judgment. To which Pietro Brucato replied, "A father hurts his own family to win a friend." To which a big-mouthed Neapolitan, who retaliated in a shotgun style, replied that Pietro should take a swim at the bottom of a coal mine, choke on the dust of his mother's grave, and may a dog shit on his tombstone.

Sensing that there was no end to this discussion, Father Antonino declared, "We put," his voice turned soft, gentle, and reverent, "San Gennaro and San Mauru in the basement tonight and tomorrow start to figure this mess out." Many, exhausted by the confrontation, started home. However, the most intractable supporters of San Gennaro, who argued that his blood liquefies and his intervention deflects the lava of volcanoes, argued that they would keep the money the saint made today, which was nearly two hundred dollars, and they would deliver him to the basement landing only if given assurances that the outside door to the basement would be locked to save their new patron from destruction and kidnapping. The supporters of San Mauru, not to be outdone, insisted that the inside door be locked so, they said with sarcasm, San Gennaro couldn't find the stairs and put himself on the altar.

For Father Antonino the battle was as unintelligible as it was ridiculous and spiteful. And all this was magnified by the irrepressible thought, "I studied Christian theology for years to minister to petty and warring pagan villagers?" More simply, his parishioners' exaggerated piety had for him no place in the teaching of either Paul, Augustine, Bonaventura, or others, and it seemed he would sacrifice his life ministering to what he called magical pagan materialists. Both a second glass of wine or a reading of a serious theologian, or the two in combination, sharpened the edge of his self-interrogation and added to a mood of irony about self and disdain of others that had gnawed at him since he first loved the Christ of humble ministry and the Saint Paul of reasoned faith.

An hour later, with San Gennaro and San Mauru safely locked in the basement, the crowd dispersed. Father Antonino stood alone on the front steps of the church, tired, saddened, trying to digest what had just occurred. On this still, windless, starry summer night, when the skies were so firmly in place and orbit, he was visibly shaken. His head turned like a top. Gyrating within, he was thinking everything and nothing at the same time. He was sure that he had just met the first chapter of a long painful book, which held episode upon episode of mean divisions and gnashing of teeth.

He had come prepared to have all join their suffering to Christ's. He had hoped to offer his people and himself to redemption. In town only a few hours, he now faced a full-scale war between two saints and Sicilian and Neapolitan parishioners. Father Antonino's musings were interrupted on the steps of the church by Joseph Bruno, a man in his early fifties, dressed in a black suit. Joseph Bruno politely approached Father Antonino and invited him to his home for a glass of wine and "a little something to eat." With a wry, sly smile and a wink, he suggested that perhaps he could provide "a more fitting introduction (*un'introduzione piu guista*)—to Kelayres and the Immaculate Conception Parish. Father Antonino accepted.

An hour later, into his third glass of Bruno's homemade Zinfandel, he found himself all too at home with Bruno. He was too light-headed to consider, which in the back of his mind he knew he should, why he should be saying so much to a man he knew so little.

Combing his silver hair back, alternately with his right and then left hand, as if to massage his words, Bruno interrupted Father Antonino frequently to offer him more wine or a special Italian *dolci* he had just brought from Newark. The old man cast a nimbus of attentive reverence around the young priest as he asked Father Antonino who he was, what he wanted out of life, and what he expected from his first assignment at Immaculate Conception. Beyond his solicitous interrogation, Bruno depicted himself as standing beyond, and above, the foibles of his fellow parishioners. And with humorous anecdotes thrown in here and there about this or that parishioner, he left no doubt about his condescension and scarcely veiled his arrogant disdain for both the camp of San Gennaro and that of San Mauru. Were they both not superstitious, "our lambs" who must be fed and cared for? On this point, Father Antonio took Bruno's manner of speech to be a quaint and ornate old Sicilian way of speaking. He took its deeper intention to confide the care of the parishioners into the new priest's hands.

When Father Antonino tried to broach directly the subject of what Joseph Bruno saw lying ahead in the parish struggle, Bruno said, "It is late. It is time for us to go to bed. The morning sun will bring the new day." He then quickly added, "You will sleep here tonight. You can leave the rectory for tomorrow night and seven following years. On our pillows you will have sweet dreams—at our table you will get your morning panini with the best oil." Before Father Antonino had digested Joseph Bruno's words, Bruno's wife,

Carmella, was fluffing up the pillows on the guest's bed, putting water on the night stand, giving him a new pair of pajamas, and wishing him goodnight, "*Buona notti.*"

Morning did come—and it meant an icy meeting with the new housekeeper, Giuseppina Perna. Father Antonino had ignored all her preparations by sleeping and eating breakfast at the Brunos. Before he could dwell on his errors a parade of parishioners came. They brought gifts of all sorts—cakes, holy pictures, postcards, a bucket of coal, and stamps off letters they had received from the old country. Assuming that he would garden and raise animals behind the rectory, parishioners presented him with seeds, stakes for his tomatoes, chicks, and a new shovel and hoe. Bachelor Giovanni, who spent all the time he could in the woods, gave him a handmade map, which indicated the best blueberry patches in the hills up behind the adjacent town of McAdoo. Two individuals came for confession, believing only a young virgin priest could forgive their wicked deeds. The first confessed the rape of a sister-in-law and the second the murder of a friend in a fight years ago. One couple came to make their marriage plans. A sister asked Father Antonino to go to the old stone prison in Pottsville to visit her brother who had killed their abusive father ten years ago. A mother asked Father Antonino to go to the Byberry Asylum to visit her daughter, who one day decided she was a witch and ran away to the woods to be with her boyfriend and to seek plants for magic love potions.

At the end of this first long day, two small groups of men appeared in the waiting room. Wearing their Sunday best, which meant shabby and musty suits and muddy shined shoes, with a mixture of nervous, clumsy, and assertive gestures, they announced who they were, which Father knew the moment he saw them. He had no doubt that they represented sides taken on behalf of the feuding saints. As if his mind had been preparing him all day long for this meeting, without hesitation, he invited both groups into his large parlor. He made them comfortable by calling the housekeeper to pour wine and coffee, and then he promptly took control of the meeting. "Let's begin! What good can we make out of these two saints?"

Surprising himself as much as the quarreling sides, Father Antonino offered a proposal. "Yes, we will move San Gennaro to the left side of the altar in a position similar to that which San Mauru holds on the right. We will make a special place for displaced Saint Joseph, God bless him, at the back of the church." And, yes, the Sicilians' mouths already opened dropped all the way as Father Antonino went on to say, "We will have an annual procession for San Gennaro in the fall and we will continue our summer procession for San Mauru." Silence momentarily ruled in the wake of having given one group more than it imagined and taken from the other group all it feared. He continued: "The hearts of a large part of the parish must not go unfulfilled. No matter what has been, we must allow all to profess their devotion fully." However, as an afterthought he swept both groups completely off their feet by proposing that money earned by both professions will be given to the parish, with only a return of ten percent each to the Sicilians' Sons of Italy Chapter and the Neapolitans' *Filge di San Gennaro*. Father Antonino abruptly ended the meeting, in contradiction to the expectation of its participants, who anticipated it would drag on for hours. He concluded, "Go away and discuss my proposal and come back with your responses next Saturday."

To an eerie silence, barely compromised by a cough or a whining child, Father Antonino repeated his proposal, which was understood to be his ruling, in his Sunday homily to more than a hundred parishioners at nine o'clock mass. They filed out of church as defendants justly sentenced to what was beyond appeal. They didn't like what Father Antonino proposed but he—such a young priest—had ruled and left no alternative.

During the following days, the dusty streets of Kelayres, on which men traditionally gathered in the evening after supper to roll their bocce balls and take a walk, were mainly empty. Trumping up errands, many went out in hopes of finding a conversation, which never came about. The porches on both sides of Front Street were waiting for something to occur that never happened. Julietta, the most anxious woman in town, kept asking, "*Pirchi nessunu parla? Pirchi?*"

On Friday Nunzio Mutaccio cracked the silence ruling on the streets of Kelayres. In the middle of a bocce game, he declared out of the blue: "It's our money. No priest should have it." As if a dam had broken, everyone, even the most taciturn of the Sicilians, chipped in his two cents. Irrespective of whether they were on the side of one saint or the other, men in unison affirmed the belief, "It is our money and we should spend it as our saint wishes." Even those who rarely participated in the procession of the saints and never once in their life pinned a dollar on any saint, joined their voices to complaining choruses. The biggest bawler, Giovanni Scarpati, shouted, "We should support the saint who supports us." Women on the porch joined in, "We dress them and undress them, and we should keep the money they make." Rosalia Pellagallo declared in a high and shrill voice her own invented proverb, which all admired, "A saint without pants has empty pockets."

For one magical hour the supporters of San Mauru and the followers of San Gennaro, in debt for their new statue, were in perfect agreement. They stood shoulder to shoulder in advocating that each group receive the lion's share of money made by the saint. This included all the money that the saint brought in, in addition to funds made from the saint day's fair and dinner, and the accompanying drinking, gambling, and dancing that went with the festival. The parish should receive only ten percent of the proceeds.

Despite all the rousing and buoying words, the town awoke deflated. It was as if sleep were a leak. It had drained each and every person of his enthusiasm to battle the new young priest, who they knew would have the money-hungry bishop behind him. The clerical grip on money is tight. The delegations to the priest went resigned in their defeat at the hands of Father Antonino. The followers of San Gennaro and San Mauru mechanically recited their "Yes, father," as if agreeing to Easter penance after spending a year of hard sinning. Father Antonino had nipped his parish conflict in the bud and had become a lasting object of universal resentment. As long as he served at Immaculate Conception, he would be the priest who had imposed an unwanted peace. Aside from a handful of reflexive pious priest-lovers, Father Antonino would not be loved.

So, reversing all he wished and planned, his first parish assignment isolated him and drove him inward toward the meditative life. All this made him welcome the frequent invitations to the Brunos', where he would be fed, drink more wine than was appropriate (especially given he would be drinking the blood-wine of the Savior the following morning), and unburden his soul to his haughty host as if he himself were giving a long-pent-up confession. He found himself repeatedly revealing things about himself and divulging too much about others. As much as he enjoyed the chance to give his tongue free rein, regret and remorse predictably followed his evenings at the Brunos'. As much as he swore he would never again accept Joseph Bruno's invitations, he spontaneously accepted each invitation, and remorse set in only after his second or third glass of Bruno's Zinfandel.

He analyzed his behavior frequently and found his principal motivations primarily one: he was lonely and, more than he ever knew, he needed to be one with others. However, in addition to good food and drink, there was the magnetic personality of Joseph Bruno. The old man listened to the young priest as if he were the priest's confessor. In turn, old man Bruno spiced his conversations with wit. Under the guise of gentle humor and self-deprecation, Bruno incised the failures and evils of all with short and crisp chisel strokes, which reminded Father Antonino of the artfully carved portraits of the saints that so appealed to him.

Something else attracted Antonino to old Bruno. The young priest could not quite put his finger on it, but he could not deny how much he enjoyed listening to Joseph when with name and precise description of his craft, he described how he and his gang in Kelayres and McAdoo controlled the Township through the local chapter of the Republican Party centered on the Schuylkill Court House in Pottsville. His web of connections equaled money and jobs, keys to power, especially during these Depression days. At his most animated and revealing, Bruno told how he stole the '32 election. He detailed lining up the teachers and county workers he had gotten jobs and the poor and widows who received deliveries of coal and groceries, and fees for voting. When his three "boys," young men in their twenties, were present, old Bruno lost his reticence altogether, bragging and joking about how being a Bruno is to out-think all the other *Neri*. At these moments, Father Antonino felt compelled to chide him with gentle exhortation about democracy and respect. Bruno conceded that his words had carried him beyond what was right and apologized for his desire to get "more than his fair share." The young priest accepted the old man's transparent apologies and counterfeit repentance and let him proceed weaving his guileful web of duplicity and cleverness.

After spending an especially long evening with old man Bruno Father Antonino, as never before, was remorseful about his complicit sinfulness. He sensed that he had sullied himself. On that morning, for no other reason than what he called grace, he prayed the Confiteor and the Kyrie of the day's mass extra loud and made it a confession worthy of the communion he would take. Beyond his own will Father Antonino found himself drawing away from the snare of Joseph Bruno and the Bruno den. The more he withdrew the freer he felt.

Indeed, less than two months from his decision to quit the Brunos, the full evil of Brunos burst forth one evening. A small group of county Democrats had already paraded earlier that week in Kelayres with placards declaring that they would not let the Brunos and the Republicans steal this election as they had stolen the election in 1932. Now again, with the same placards, a crowd of more than three hundred undertook a torchlight parade through the streets of Kelayres. When they had almost reached one of the two Bruno family houses and were almost directly across from Immaculate Conception, a fusillade exploded.

Shots seemed to burst from every direction. In an instant they sheared the parade into a hundred pieces. Those who didn't fall dead or wounded fled. They hid in bushes, cowered behind porches, and ran down alleys. Howls of pain and shouts of anguish, supplications and lamentations, were sent up. And they were increasingly mixed with savage imprecations and curses against the Brunos. Many were wounded and six were dead before they reached the Hazelton hospital by private cars. One died shortly after arriving.

Among the dead, who were all males, was a handsome young Slavic man from McAdoo, Daniel Slavek, a father of three young children, who had been shot in the back. Father Antonino, who had been among the first to rush out onto the streets to minister to the fallen, tried to cradle the head of the large young man in his arms, as his body twitched and lurched until it was still and he was dead. Amid the mayhem of a street filled with fear and horror, and then howls and screams, and then mumbled words in hushed silence, Father Antonino had stared into the panic-filled eyes of the young man he held until they lost their light and became as cold and empty as a freezing winter night. The words of his prayers felt like stones dropped down a deep well.

Father Antonino heard but did not take in the meaning of the shout, "Make way, Slavek's wife is coming; she is on the way!" until she had arrived in trembling flesh and threw herself prostrate, wailing, on the chest of the man whose head he cradled. Long minutes later he helped lift her from her dead husband and guided this broken and depleted woman—this freshly made widow—into the waiting arms of her gathered relatives. He then nodded to the undertaker D'Amico, who had stood to the side, with hands crossed and head bowed, to advance and take away the body, and he proceeded to the other dead and wounded.

The priest, who slept that night in his clothes, awoke with the knees of his pants stiff with blood and a head filled with throbbing anger. He hated the Brunos. He hated them for befriending him, for feeding him, for counseling him, and, worse, for having revealed to him their arrogance and political manipulation. He detested the web Joseph had spun and hated the father who incited his sons not just to a family murder, as a mobster might, but open and random slaughter of those who opposed them! Here was the wolf among the sheep. But as much as he hated Bruno, he hated himself more. He, the shepherd, had helped write the wolf's menu.

Conscience pushed Father Antonino to visit each family of the dead and wounded. He felt he must be among his people in their time of need. All asked why God and San Mauru and San Gennaro allowed this tragedy to occur. Some welcomed him—and even leaned on him for support. Others only out of politeness tolerated him. One family openly rejected him and hissed at him as he left their front steps. "A friend of our enemies does not bury our dead." (*"Un amicu dei nostri nemici non si sepulta i nostri morti."*) The bullet of their sentence lodged at the base of Father Antonino's heart. Unforgettable and not allayed by prayer, every time he remembered the insult, he shuddered as if freshly wounded.

The memory of what became known as the Kelayres Massacre reminded him of the time, when a boy, trapped in a revolving door at Wanamakers Department Store in Philadelphia, he went round and round, never consoling and never being consoled. Then he recalled how once when a very young boy he got locked in a dark basement filled with manikins, which he took to be dead zombies. His dreams were worse. In one he was trapped in an elevator operated by Joseph Bruno. Seated on a little stool, along the side of the controls, to which he firmly held, old man Bruno was dressed in a red uniform with gold braided epaulettes and a crowning bellhop cap—and, with great jerks between floors, he shuttled Antonino up and down from a dark cavernous shaft below to a swaying tower on high. Stopping at random floors, at which groups of people drank, danced, and laughed, and wept and huddled around coffins, Bruno refused to let the young priest off. When Antonino tried to break out of the elevator, old Bruno, snarling, held tight to the gate, which instantly metamorphosed into the bars of the prison cell that held Bruno and his sons. With festive laughs, sneering and aiming their rifles, they mocked Antonino's efforts to free himself from the cell and forced him to drink wine and eat cream-stuffed cannoli after cannoli.

Saying mass, listening to confessions, or even visiting the dead young man's widow, to whom he had become increasingly attached, did not relieve the gloom that shrouded his days. As much as he loved her voice and animated speech and graceful movement and relished the chance to play with her children, his conscience painfully warned: as his relationship with the Brunos betrayed him to evil, might not his ministry to the widow mask his coveting flesh?

As much as he prayed to God, his gloom did not lift. Work in his garden, long walks along the train tracks and berry picking in the nearby hollow, playing on the local softball team, and even occasional trips to Newark (to visit an old friend in seminary) offered no relief. He found no consolation in theology, and the predictable content on despair and sin caused him to throw more than one book down. The only books that provided him some pleasure were travel books on Sicily; in them, he focused on picturesque scenes of mountain villages, seaside towns, and the remains of old Greek, Roman, Arab, and Norman civilizations. But even these photographs, especially those of the lamenting Madonna and young women wearing black, turned his mind to the widow he consoled and yet courted.

He prayed daily that grace would remove the bullet lodged at the bottom of his heart and that God himself would care for the dead and their relatives. He repeated the same sermons to himself over and over again that he must not let the present drown in the past—in the Lord's words, "Let the dead bury the dead." But his preachment fell flat. He could not forgive himself his betrayal: he had not spared his people suffering but afflicted them with it.

The parishioners of Kelayres took the measure of his worsening condition. Those with sympathy and pity for Father Antonino said the massacre yesterday was killing him today. "Our curse has become his curse." "Oh, how heavy things weigh on him. The dance has gone out of his step, and he now trudges like an old man."

Proposed cures ran the gamut; they included a proposal for long vacations, be it to the Poconos or New York or Florida or one-day trips to churches at Scranton, Wilkes Barre, and even Audenreid, just a few coal banks away from Kelayres and where once the notorious Molly McGuires conspired. Some advised retreats. Others suggested additional Sunday morning bell ringing—fourteen rather than seven gongs, they proposed; while yet others, who conceived of the cure of everything only a garden or kitchen away, proposed hanging rings of garlic, mixing olive oil and almonds, chopping up rats' liver, and any of a number of other ingredients used to defeat the evil eye. Some out of habit called for prayers to impotent San Mauru, while the parish's crazy old Ukrainian advised the curative powers of Wednesday night bingo in Tamaqua. Old Toto brought more than one evening conversation about Father Antonino to a close by declaring, "Every sailor needs a port."

The bishop, never without a tattletale or two, was not ignorant of Father Antonino's condition, and he decided the time to intervene had come. An ardent baseball fan himself, the bishop had decided Father Antonino now had three strikes on him. His artful handling of the war of the saints had, nevertheless, cost him the affection of the majority of his parishioners. His tainting friendship with the Brunos had made him a target for expulsion from Kelayres by at least a quarter of the parishioners. And now, his growing relationship with the widow, on the one hand, and his intractable depression, on the other, assuredly would end, if he were not removed, by scandalizing the whole church. With this in mind, the bishop tactfully penned a careful letter to Father Antonino, offering him a chance for additional study in Rome starting in the fall or a near-immediate assignment to a small chapel at the naval base in Pearl Harbor, Hawaii.

Rome and the chance it offered for study and its closeness to Sicily attracted Father Antonino. But the idea of instantly leaving with a pious reason to say goodbye to the widow attracted him even more. Two weeks later he boarded a plane on the first leg of a trip to Hawaii. During the next six years, Father Antonino slowly learned to forgive himself. The marriage of the widow eased missing her as did the good will and healing wishes expressed in their final letters. He developed friends on and off the base, and knowing what loneliness meant, he counseled the sailors well.

On a typical Sunday morning, December 7, 1941, as he prepared to say nine o'clock mass, waves of Japanese attack planes began the bombardment. Alongside of burning and smoking ships, he administered last rites to many seamen. Ships rolled over and sank, ending one age and beginning another. A new war of saints had begun—and he did not conceive that in the service of American troops he would die a year and half later of malaria administering to infantry in Sicily. He would be buried on the outskirts of the base hospital of Cefalù at foot of the Madonie Mountains. He would be disinterred and returned to his mother, who had left Sicily fifty years before for America.

PART TWO

Poems

I. SITES AND CITIES

Voceria in Vucceria

In Palermo's market,
The *Vucceria*,
A *Voceria*—
Voices,
Basses and tenors—
Amid stands and carts of food
Bark and holler and chant.

Their haunting scale
Calls me back to my youth
In Detroit.
Lawns browned,
And hydroplanes
With airplane engines roared,
Slapping,
Plowing up and down the city's great choppy river
With a humming churn and an air-born shrill whine.

It was then
In late summer's full heat
Fruit peddlers came
In red trucks.
With canvas awnings
Rolled up on both sides
And a blaring microphone,
They sang out
Their green fare
As if in a Palermo market
Or at the top of an Arab minaret.

Sweee-eet peas
Eass,
Pota tooo
Es
Andd straaaaww
Ahh
Berrrr
Ies."

The sugar
Of red
Chanted us awake
To the summer's sweetest
Passing days.

A Balcony in Palermo

I have no perch
Other than my walking feet
And turret-turning head.
I cannot but look around,
Tourist that I am.

What is the holding strength
Of that wrought-iron
Balcony?
I ask
As the turn of its Baroque curve
Invites the flop of the generous breasts
Pointing down
Like their possessor's omniscient stare
Without promise of tenderness
Onto the rushing traffic
Of these Jurassic streets.

Here are the shallows
Of the market,
Where fruits and vegetables
Attract
And hawkers
Of beads and purses
And other right and little things
Search a day's meal
And night's sleep in unlit barracks
In the dark sweat of their own kind.

I am the tourist
Who has come to see all,

Who sees nothing
And is desperate for a single self-clinching thought
That will fly me up
High, forever,
Above the cage of self
Beyond this Sicilian ground
That earthquakes rake
And seas pound.

What truth can I proclaim
Beyond and above all adjectival lists,
True beyond all disputed cases,
Free of quarreling antinomies,
Loud, rude
Street pleadings?

Moroccan Market in Palermo

Moroccans,
The meanest of merchants,
Occupy Palermo's streets.
They arrange purses
And straighten jewelry
And beads
All day,
Itching the small sale,
All to huddle at night
With a full stomach
Amid familiar smell and speech.
Under the frame of Sicilian oak rafters
They will dream stars
That jeweled mountain skies
And the sparkle of dark eyes
Of the pearled dancing girls
With alluring ruby lips
And swinging, tightly clothed hips
Rocking, swaying, swinging
Rhythmically,
Frantically,
Orgiastically,
In luxuriant tents
By the desert's oasis waters.

Memories in Geraci

On the periphery
Of Geraci, Sicily,
A passing, rumbling cement truck
Calls me home
To the east side of Detroit,
Where we Sicilians
Who worked with cement and stone
Were not satisfied with well-manicured grass.
We dressed ourselves in the cloth of stone.
Fieldstone faced our homes;
Carefully laid and decorated paving stone
Formed walkways
Through gardens
Abloom with yellow, white, and red roses,
And trellises
Of vines and flowers,
Violet and pink.

We erected plaster shrines to St. Francis,
Always clothed in brown;
And the Virgin,
Placid in white,
Was caped in blue.
Nearby birdbaths welcomed all,
The feathered cavorting
Of common brown sparrows
And the solemn hop
Of a full-dress robin.

Gardens and cemeteries
With their mausoleums

Housed us—
Life and memory in stone.
The crafting hand
Joined us to the rock gardens
Of this ancient land.

Geraci Morning

In a little park
Behind the public fountain,
In the shadow of the commanding
Ventimiglia Castle,
Which centuries ago
Ruled the converging and fertile valleys below,
A cat walks across the lawn,
Breaking the starry crystals
Of morning dew.

Blood in a Rose Baptismal Font

Four lions facing
In the cardinal directions
Decorate the outer rim
Of the rose baptismal font
In Cefalù Cathedral.

Font of blessings and amens,
Its stone is iron-dyed by Jurassic seas
And rich in ammonites
Whose shells grew
In a spiral swell
Of ever larger chambers
Housing life's first specialized organs:
Ammonites
That swam the same seas
As prehistoric sharks—*squali!*—
Cutting cruel swathes
Across mean red seas.

Erected under the icon of Christ Pantocrator,
The iconic stamp of Norman sovereignty over Sicily,
This font for a thousand years
To this day
Has washed away the stain of Original Sin,
Elevating canine-toothed man above
The descent of Darwin.

But as I peer down into this rose font,
Sharks still hunt—
And, with a fearful mind,
I pray for my kind.

In Enna at Seventy-Five

Late in life,
I come to high-castled Enna,
The protruding navel of Sicily
Anchored
At the center of the earth's sea,
The Mediterranean.

In morning light I scope the round:
To the north Italy and Europe,
To the south shadowing Africa,
To the east other islands and Greece,
And to the near west the Madonie Mountains
That my grandparents left
For what the new land promised
And the ancient denied.

In the long shadow of midday
I meet mother goddess Demeter,
Who assured spring's grain,
And her daughter, Persephone,
Who carried out the curses of the living
Against the dead
And turned blasphemers' bones
To heaps of stone.

Still molten with life,
I own my kinship
With nearby Etna.
Ringed in clouds,
Her snow-covered cone
Fumes,

Tosses rocks into the sky,
Gurgles,
Stands ready to spew
Fiery rivers
Down its sides.

Enna tonight
Is that blessed night
When my grandparents took flight.
Ignorant stars shined bright,
Making a sublime canopy
Over our family's unforeseen
Circus history.

Enna in May

In the pitted walls
Of palaces and churches,
Pigeons roost,
Conspire
With hushed,
Climaxed,
And then, subsiding cooing.
Satisfied,
They fly off,
Indifferent to walls
Of cascading wild flowers—
Redolence of red, yellow,
Purple, and pink—
That make May abundant
And spring generous.

Enna Is Center

I make Enna my compass,
Its highest tower
My eye's gyre.

Umbilico del mondo,
Enna centers Sicily,
Which bobs and floats
In the Mediterranean,
Born in the Jurassic
And named the center
Of the earth.

Sicily, unresolved duality
Of earth and sea,
Things below and above.
To the south, Africa,
Whence bipedal man trod.
To the east Greece, Egypt, and the Near East,
From which civilizations flowed
With their imperial and celestial
Hegemonies and sovereignties.

To the north young Europe
With its two thousand years
Of mischief.
And to the North and West,
Normans, Sabines, Spaniards,
And the Americas.

Here in Enna
Space mutates into time.

History becomes the labyrinth
Of the homeless,
And yesterday sums today,
And tomorrow multiplies and recalculates
Yesterday.

May Flowers Top Greek Vases

I was delighted today
To discover that Enna's museum was shut.
My mind has been cut too often
By razor-thin black obsidian flakes
And stabbed too often
By Bronze Age blades.

I have lost my equilibrium
Once too often
To Gravettian hips and breasts,
And I no longer yearn
To peer through clean glass
At another Greek urn.

Forgive me, Keats—
Truth is not beauty;
A Greek vase
Does not equal
A living face,
Flesh to touch,
Especially when May flowers bloom
And their color and scent race
In this old man's blood.

A Farm Building Made a Restaurant in Castelbuono

Walls, doors, and floors,
Crescendo of textures and colors
Conducted by the day's setting sun,
Made symphonic by the faces of changing seasons,
And finished works,
Opere complete,
By family fortunes.
Vases, jugs, and barrels
In corners, along walls,
At the sides of doorways,
And along courtyard ledges
Round off lines,
Cast harmonizing shadows,
And present sun-bright
Bouquets of flowers
Brick-orange,
Rose-red,
Tan and yellow,
Purple and blue
As the soul's prism.

Swallow by the Wall

A single fallen swallow
Lies at the base of a wall
With one wing gracefully stretched out
And head twisted about.
With smallest, beady, interrogating eye
It asks: Now you, pedestrian, zigzag by,
But when will you too fall from the sky
And die,
Alone?
The world is big,
And we are small flesh,
All.

At Morgantina

In eastern Sicily
More than five centuries before the saving Christ,
Field-rock roads
Routed by carts
Ran straight
Through undulating fields of tall grass.

On the east end of the site
Relentless digging archaeologists uncover pipes
For baths and laundries,
Pools and tubs,
That soaked and scoured
Bodies and clothes clean
Of long sweaty days.

On the northwest corner
Sits a curved amphitheater
Carved into a hillside
Facing the sea.
On its stage
Actors charted distant journeys
With choirs of cathartic words,
Telling of the sensuous snare
Of Helen's beauty,
Troy's glorious temporality,
Of aged father Priam
Pleading with proud Achilles
For son Hector's body.

The choir repeats
The shared fate of skin and bone

Below this sun
With its shimmering light
And through the tunnel
Of dream-filled nights.

Sperlinga

1

Where mountains and valleys crisscross,
And exposed beds steeply slant,
There is the castle town,
Sperlinga.

Its genesis,
The fertility of fields below.
Its strength and security,
A fusion of mountain rock and man-made walls.

Its roads and ramps quarrel
Their way up and down
To and from the castle's gates,
Passing thick private doors,
Now largely gone to rot
But constantly reminding that treasures
Are forever down and in,
And locked up.

Rounded by age's wear
And cut and creased
By geology's rip and tear,
Sperlinga belongs too
To the wash and suck
Of distant histories
That reach even these mountain-high Sicilian shores.

2

Declining the castle's promise
Of a panoramic view,
I held below
To the coffee bar,
Where I envied an old shepherd's walking stick
Of wild pear,
A divining stick
For going out
And looking about.

I searched the lower quarters
That draped down the backside
Of this town's dark and grey heights
And found that they were stitched and seamed
By patches of wild flowers
And held sunlit gardens
So small, so bright,
Convincing me—
Assuring all!—
That light
Came before
Rock and wall,
And growing green spawned colors,
Bugs, fish, birds, and all that creeps and runs
In and out of cool shadows.

Piazza Armerina

1

I am walking on the upper roadway
To the Villa Imperiale de Casale, Sicily,
A governing lord's hunting and bathing resort
Containing a wealth of floors and walls
Of mosaics of men and women at work and play
And animals from all over the known world
Hunted, captured, put in harness,
And run wild in the circus of Roman imagination.

I stop with a startle:
At my feet,
A black snake
Twists, writhes
To wiggle and worm itself free
Of its skin,
Which gathers black flies and golden wasps.

How hard it is to escape
The old skin of our sins
And return to fresh grass
And spring's wild flowers.

2

Resuming my buoyant step
Towards Casale's entrance,
Moved by expectation,
I hear a clarion invitation—
The seventeen-hundred-year-old

Patrician of the Casale commands:
"Do not resist my generosity.
Come for a stay at my deluxe hunting lodge."

At the front door,
Slave hands will bathe you
And scrape your skin.
You will be submerged in pools
Of hot and cool waters.

Then comes a soothing rest:
You will be sensually knotted in fleshy beds,
Curled around the pleasurable rounds of breasts, thighs,
And big fleshy buttocks.

In other quarters:
Lighter and thin athletic women
In tight two-piece garments
Of colorful tops and scanty bottoms
Do tricks.
They prance and dance,
Toss red balls,
And wave palms.
Come.
Resume your walk on these mosaic floors,
Around the outer perimeters
And through the inner halls.
You will be made prisoner
Of this palace's chambered pleasure,
Made to marvel by the geometer's shaping eye
And the ceramicists' intricate patterns of loops and bends.

My mosaics
Are galleries
Of imagination.
They will cup and swirl your mind in images

Of hunt,
Capture,
Taming.
They will ring you in a circus
Of friend-enemy-fellow-creatures.
Animal and beast,
Horned and fanged,
Hair-covered and skin-nude,
Winged,
With padded paws and razor-sharp claws,
Ready to pounce
Already satiated in blood and bone.
So they will pose before you life-like
In colored stone.

I caution you,
Before you enter a long corridor
Leading to chambers of rest,
Some cups on leaning tables
Have venomous potions:
They taste of hurting and biting relations,
Of hurting selves,
And mixes of coarse bile
And subtle guile.
You know how we humans are.

In love's cloisters
You will see row upon row
Of variety and feast:
Head of beast next to hind of beast,
Chariots pulled by harnessed birds
And carts by whipped oxen.
Ships at dockside
Are collecting beasts
From all dominions,
From India to Africa.

Carried, tugged, goaded, and pulled on board,
They fill a ship's hold
And a Roman collector's menagerie
And luxurious curiosity.

On the floor of the banquet room
Elephants and striped tigers,
Great-winged geese and wild bulls parade,
Beside which hippopotamuses and camels march,
Porpoises and swordfish dive and swim,
And a cornered wild boar seeks to gore
The hunter's hounds.

Indeed, I hope you see everything.
Appreciate what my craftsmen know:
The unity of the many,
The variety of the one
Are joined in beauty.

And please don't overlook the single black serpent
That slithers on one tile
Or the four on a ceiling frame,
Which have roped themselves
Around a man and woman,
With their heads and fangs poised to strike and bite.

In the end, you, my invited one,
Must recognize:
No place or palace,
However ostensibly natural and bright,
Is without a black serpent,
A house snake.

In Agrigento

In Agrigento,
A plateau
On the southern shore of Sicily
Where two rivers,
The Hypas and Akragas,
Join the sea,
Temples sorted out the fates
Of gods and peoples.
.

In the nearby Greek colony of Gela,
The tyrant Phalaris
Made an immense bronze bull,
And in the great hollow cavity of its stomach
He boiled his enemies alive
And made them the fare
Of a city feast.

Today,
I, whose grandparents were chased by poverty
And fled with wings of wish,
Stand in a field of bright light
In the long thin valley
Of eastward-facing temples
In which old Greek gods
Awoke to the day
By drinking rising sunlight
And ate human hearts
In the day's heat.

I enter the dank and clanging hold
Of my grandparents' iron clattering steamship.

I join them in the once-in-a-lifetime trip they took
To enter a Pennsylvania anthracite mine
Then place themselves
Amidst the blue sparks
And press and grind
Of a Detroit auto factory
To gather a family
Around a red-and-white-checkered oilcloth
With plates of pasta
And red sauce
For a meal not to be shared
Free of temple priests
And light-drinking and flesh-sucking gods.

II. Family Fortunes

Dancing with My Grandparents

My grandparents
Came from families
Without a donkey to mortgage,
A garden for tillage.

They came to America
With arms to work,
Backs to bend,
Wombs to conceive,
And hands to clasp
In hope.

Grandfather Antonino
Came first down out of the hills
Of the western border of the *Madonie,*
Following the descending *Rio Torto,*
Ambiguously translated as
The curving, the mistaken, the hurting river.

A young man of twenty-five,
Antonino followed the river
Down to the sea
For the first time in his life
And went west along its northern coast,
Passing below the auspices of Santa Rosalia
And through the shadows of Mount Pellegrino
To the nearby port of Palermo
Humming with the coming and going
Of scheduled steamships
That delivered mountaineers, peasants, and villagers,
Smelly shepherds and stinky goat herders

Noi siciliani tutti
To American shores
From the old country's rocky ground
Fit to grow neither farm nor family.

He crossed the sea
For the coal mines
Of Pennsylvania,
Anthracite region.
After going down into the mine one day,
He worked for three years
Above ground
In a grocery store
In a coal village, Kelayres,
Named after two Irish owners,
Kelly and Ayres.

Through the agency of Rosalia's brother,
Great Uncle Peter,
Antonino sent a marriage proposal
To Rosalia,
Five years his younger.

Mutually satisfied with the photos they exchanged,
Terms proposed,
From ten miles farther up
The Rio Torto,
From a rockier and steeper land
Of fewer orchards and gardens,
Rosalia came
To Pennslyvania.

They were married,
Rosalia quickly conceived,
And within the year
They moved to Detroit
 Booming with opportunities.

Four years later,
With things starting to go his and Rosalia's way,
Antonino came home sick
From the factory one day.
Suffering through the night,
He was dead
By morning's light
Of a burst appendix.

He was dead,
Like Christ,
At thirty-three
And buried in a large eastside cemetery,
Mount Olivet,
At the top of a small knoll
Surrounded by immigrants
From Poland, Ireland, and Italy.

Under the shadows of Chryslers,
He left grandmother Rosalia widowed
With one child in her womb
And another clutching her hand,
My father, not quite three.
And then there was the memory
She could not bury
In that boiling scrub bucket
That scalded their first child
To death.

Her lament,
As old as tragedy itself,
Hollowed the family
From Sicily
And dressed it in black
All its American days,
Except at white and florid Easter,

When my Irish mother prompted Rosalia
Out of her black dress.

Oh, but with the wish
Of memory's kiss,
I would have Antonino alive again
As he never was
To my father and me—
Have him become more than a betrothal photo
Of a square-shouldered and square-jawed man
Handsome on a lace doily
On Rosalia's dresser,
More than a ghostly flicker
Of a red votive candle.

I would hear the cackle of his Sicilian,
Taste his Zinfandel,
Hear him command me:
"Chidete.
Non parlare più!
Mangia!"
"Shut up! Eat!"

Embrace him once,
For the first time ever,
See his sun- and factory-worn hands,
Watch him cradle my Joe,
Dead at seventy-seven
Twenty-five years ago,
And sister Fina,
Whom he never saw.

In my prayers,
He dances his best wedding dance
With my Rosalia,
And we travel back up the slopes
Of bending Rio Torto

With Rosalia on my left
And Antonino on my right
In the season
When gardens are in full bloom
And wild flowers flourish.

Then I would shut up
And eat my heart's fill
Under a canopy
Of olive trees
And love.

Rosalia

Rosalia had never,
Even in her imagination,
Charted the sea
Or visited it—
Rolled up her skirt and waded and splashed
In that great flat blue sea below,
Which came and went in the village
With daylight.

Not far beyond the end
Of the long meandering path
That passed through Aliminusa and Cerda
To the great fork—
East to Cefalù
And west to Palermo—
The path turned road,
Followed the Crooked River,
Il Rio Torto,
On what would be for Rosalia
A two- or possibly three-day
Once-in-forever adventure:
Al mare e poi Palermo—
To the sea and then the great city,
The port of Palermo.

Rosalia had never before filled the sails
Of her hope
With westward winds.
She knew only
That now in her hand
Was a ticket for a steamer,

Sent by her fiancé,
And four dollars,
Rolled in the hem of her underwear—
And a chance for a new life,
To be a wife.

Ahead for Rosalia
Lay a continent of land
And unexplored fields of her own body.
She was opening its door and herself
To Antonino,
An emigrant from a nearby village
And friend of her brother.

As whistles blew,
Metal clanged,
And bunks vibrated,
She knew only
That she was going to another shore—
To the black diamond anthracite world of Pennsylvania.
There her sauce and pasta would steam and boil
And angel-white and demon-blue dreams would roil.

Uncle Sam's Fly

Uncle Sam stood in front of a window
That looked out on a small yard,
A sliver of a garden,
And the garage
That once housed the horse and cart
From which my father,
When only a boy of seven,
Sold fruit
To nearby factory workers.

Sam,
Who threw the ball hard
In our games of catch
And had survived the Italian campaign
And brought back a German Luger, flag, and helmet,
Swatted a fly
That lit on the oilcloth table cover
Among the black seeds
Of a freshly sliced
Georgia watermelon.

Out of the blue,
Sam declared that a house fly
Lives only a twenty-four-hour life.
My Uncle Jimmy,
Whose tour of infantry duty
Went from Sicily up the boot of Italy
Then over to Normandy
And finally into Germany
And tallied fourteen killed enemies,
Disagreed with Sam.

My dad did too.
But Sam stood his ground
In what proved an amicable go-around.

Sam died two years
After the debate
Over the life of a fly.
Stomach cancer
Took him prisoner
For eighteen months,
Reducing a two-hundred pound man
To a hundred,
Refusing a truce.

A Sicilian Father

My father is again reclined in his recliner.
He has reached the age of bad habits,
Constantly clearing his throat,
Twiddling his thumbs,
Insulting,
Finding fault,
Doing crossword puzzles,
And dozing off.
He is seventy.

Reclined in his recliner
He appears to be practicing dying.
His face is long and drawn,
His breath is deep,
Precarious,
Hesitant.
He sleeps as if he is without dreams.

As sons everywhere,
I am drawn to and repulsed by
My sleeping father.
Fleeing him,
I seek out the land
Of his father and mother:

In Sicily,
At the Greek temple Segesta
(Raised seven centuries before Christ)
I observed how snails,
Circular temples themselves,
Now decorate the dead, bleached-white stems
Of bent, scattered plants.

The small birds
Fly in and out
Of the roofless half-standing temple.
They treat it like a clump of trees,
Building nests on its highest ledges.

I follow the shepherd and his flock higher up,
To the amphitheater that surveys the land and sea below.
I sit on the highest row of curved stone
Among grazing sheep,
Asking what tragedies
Fed ancient Sicilian dreams.

At the Gate

At the gate
To Detroit's great cemetery,
Mount Olivet,
A grass, tree, and stone field
With two hundred thousand souls
Of my Catholic immigrant kind,
Stood my grandmother's second husband.
He was selling an array,
A vendor's uneven bouquet
Of potted flowers and American flags
For Memorial Day.

I had seen him only once before,
At a younger cousin's baptism.
That was when I was ten
And he was just out of prison.
This strange man approached me,
In the company of my father.
He presented me,
With no acknowledging words—
Not a phrase I can recall—
A large hunting knife
With a knurled purple plastic handle.

Only later did I learn
That more than a decade before
This one-eyed small peddler
From New York,
My father's stepfather,
Had been taken to court

By my strong grandmother
For molesting my dad's sister, Fina.

I cannot even now know
The cut of his deed—
How black it made Grandma Rosalia's mourning dress,
Forced Fina to early marriage,
Hardened my father's interior discipline,
Or set his three stepsisters
Dancing to the fast-stepping rhythms
Of a city and nation
Gone to war.

I remember only
The gouge I received
Hearing years later
About the cemetery man
Who, with flags and pinwheels,
Gave me
A knurled,
Purple,
Plastic-
Handled
Knife.

A Trip to a Detroit Cemetery

I wedge the door tight
With the furniture of memory,
Especially my father's reading chair,
When I visit
My native Detroit.

But I cannot close
The drafty cracks
That run the threshold
Of my mind
With rags and blankets
Of old stories.

Winds,
Time's prying and fingering thieves,
Enter my childhood
And tear out sheaves
Of its book.
They spin up
In whirlpools
Like autumn's gathered leaves

And float across seasons,
Over the high black wrought-iron fence
Of Mount Olivet Cemetery
Where my parents and grandparents,
Aunts and uncles
Lie,
Scarcely remembered,
Under submerged flat stones.

The leaves
Like migrating butterflies
Cluster and cross the east side,
Between the spokes
Of Gratiot and Jefferson Avenues,
Descending on the blocks
That lined and grid the palms
Of mind.

The leaves settle
In vacant yards and untended lots,
Where old immigrant houses
Once stood.
Blank and white,
Camouflaged among patches
Of retreating snow,
They whisper nothing,
On this grey spring day,
To charred houses
And passing figures.

From behind pieced-together rusty fences,
Mangy dogs
That sleep in the empty hulls
Of discarded cars
And the shadows of vacated premises
Bark.

They sense apparitions,
Old ethnic foreigners
Like Sicilian me,
Of Etna's ilk,
Who persist in remembering
An arcing, sparking,
Arsenal steel-making city—
And rivers

Of burning,
Running
Embers.

III. THE ALLURE OF FLORA

A Date with Ficus Macrophylia

It is May now,
And Sicily's wild mountain flowers
Are in full bloom,
Draping the whole landscape
In color,
As far as the cuckoo echoes.
But I have an urban date
On the northeastern corner
Of Palermo's Piazza Marina
With a magnificent tree.

She is a one-hundred-and-seventy-year-old
Ficus Macrophylia
I first met thirty-five years ago.
With her eye-captivating soul,
I didn't care a whit
That she has three luscious sisters
Who are rooted close by,
Nor did it matter
That her parents originally came
From Palermo's nearby *Orto Botanico*,
Where Goethe sought the primal *Urplanze*
And in 1845 they planted Ficus Macrophylia
As mere shoots from its native home Australia.

My ficus
Is a big, beguiling tree—
Of smooth and light skin,
Of ample curves
And alluring bends and bows.

From reaching limbs,
Ficus lowers curtains
Of draping and grasping roots
That fall like a woman's loosened hair,
A lover's tent
Pitched on the banks
Of palm-circled waters.

I cannot but love
This many-armed goddess
Who behind veil and screen
Carries on a sensuous century-long dance
Of tree, light, and earth.

I turn toward the ocean to go
Only to hear
A gentle whisper—
A promise:
At our next meeting,
She will take me
Of animal flesh,
Absorb me into her living mesh,
Embrace and root me
Into her green lifting plant race.

Green Holly

Along a Madonie trail,
I meet my first Sicilian holly,
No red-berried and obedient decorative Christmas wreath
We could circle in affectionate family embrace.
Haughty, impregnable,
She is draped in the armor
Of serrated and spine-tipped
Wax leaves.

A tabernacle
In unforgiving green,
She holds a cruel sacrament.
Vigilant, nasty, prickly goddess,
She stands alone,
A shelter for no animal flesh,
Offering no branch for bird
Or shadowy entrance for low-crawling
And deep-burrowing mammal.
Perennial, she stands her whole unforgiving shiny
Wax circumference,
Impenetrable.

Spurning all,
She says to me,
You will not find refuge
Here.
Travel rock, water, and deep grass with snakes,
I will not lend you a branch
To staff your ways
Nor be a compass
For your ascent and descent,

For beyond holiness and profanity,
I am a fortress of green
Not to be breached.
Reach in and see!

The Mystery of the Fig Tree

Before the frost entered the ground,
Uncle Joe, my grandmother's oldest sister Paulina's husband,
Dug a large hole
In his small backyard.
In it he laid his fig tree,
All wrapped and bundled cord and plastic.
He buried it below a mound of dirt
And the winter's snow.
In the spring he resurrected his fig tree—
Figure that!

Francesco's Garden

For more than a year,
Francesco and a friend
Gleaned shell casings
Along the Rio Torto
Left by General Patton's bombardments
On his way to fight the Germans
In Palermo.
With the money earned from scrap iron,
Francesco bought a small garden.
He made it a green raft
Of beans, artichokes, and tomatoes,
On which he floated wife Francesca
And seven children
To a new century.

No Truth Deeper

No truth deeper
Than the roots
Of vines
And trees
That join
Water, light, and green.

No truth greater
Than a stand of wild flowers
That drapes a wall
And covers a hillside
Or the marriage of greens
Of pines and palms.

No truth brighter
Than the wrinkled surface
Of an orange
Hanging between a cluster
Of wax green leaves
In morning sun.

IV. MY LAND

Sicily, Not Tuscany

Sicily is not soft and gentle Tuscany—
That refined and finely colored
Quilt of patches and squares
(Millennia of cultivated and manured land)
Laced together by rows of vines
And dignified with funeral stands
Of sentinel still cypresses.

Sicily,
My land,
Has abusive puppets
With swatting sticks,
Folk stories rich in boys who wear fish tails,
The stupidities of Saint Peter,
The lost King of Russia,
And the tangled ghosts of lost family flesh.
Prickly Sicily is a harsh land.

The wrinkled face of memory,
The callused hands of time,
Sicily is not valleys
Of green and bountiful gardens.
Its silhouette:
Upturned rock
And decaying castle towns.
Its melancholy rainbow
Of wall colors:
Faded tans and oranges,
Peeling whites and pinks,
Rotten black wood
Framing savage brick red.

Two Clocks

Two cuckoos' fluting refrain—
Cuckoo! Cuckoo!
Cuckoo! Cuckoo!—
Wakes the day
And fills the wooded hollow
With promise
Of love
Until
The clanging,
Unsynchronized
Metal thud
Of tolling bells
Tells
Of flocking sheep
Trudging their obedient ascent
Up the mountain path.

I awake to these two clocks
Every morning
In Sicily's mountains,
Realizing that the pendulum
Of work and love
Rules these days
And the ways
Of the living earth.

In the Valley of Temples

Here, in the Valley of Temples,
Where a Greek navy took land,
Where a colony took hold,
Where gods' temples sprung,
Lie fields of broken columns
Like fallen divine stone mills.
Here minds and lives
Were ground to powder.

The chthonic gods of earth
Harvest and grind no more.
Their bins once rife
With the chafe of jealousy and strife
Are empty of mercy and prophecy,
And we, who so admire those Greeks,
Look elsewhere for our daily bread
And care of our dead.

Only a Sliver of Pity

Normans, warrior conquerors and exquisite administrators,
Built three great churches in western Sicily:
One under the shadow of the island's great seaside rock
At Cefalù;
Another on the promontory Monreale,
Surveying Palermo and Conca d'Oro;
And a third at the very heart of the Golden Shell,
The Cappella Palatina
In once Arab Palermo.

The golden domes
Of these three churches
Hold a golden mosaic
Of Christ Pantocrator.
Robed in royal color,
Christ with all-seeing eyes
And two raised fingers
Blesses and judges all.

Each dome
Embodies the art and architecture
Of teams of European craftsmen
And Mediterranean slaves.
Each constitutes a single common testimony:
To the hegemony
And incontestable dominion
Of Norman rule.

The Pantocrator,
No Jesus of flesh
And Matthew's gospel,

Poses as the heavenly surrogate
Of royal power.
On the main altar
No miracles occur
Except the sacraments.

Daughters of Sicily,
Women long-dressed in black,
Take heed:
This Christ
Of piercing countenance
Affirms justice,
Not mercy.
Suffering women of Sicily,
Expect only a sliver of pity
From this Lord above.

Rosaries on the Beach

I sit high above the blue
Of Cefalù.
Below my balcony,
Fishermen mend their nets,
Tourists gaze,
While my host sisters
At the convent
Round the beads
Of their rosaries.

In the nearby golden-domed cathedral,
Christ Pantocrator
Is placid,
Wearing the face of Norman and heavenly rule.

In his cold iconic heights,
This lord of colored ceiling ceramics
Looms remote
With promise
Only of just and final judgment.

Two fingers raised,
With see-through eyes,
This high-seated Christ,
Elevated far beyond the shadowy corners
Lit by flickering candles,
Does not heed
A mother's imploring beads.
Annexed to power,
Its way,
Its display,

He is iconic,
Aesthetic—
Deaf
To pity,
Dumb
Of mercy.

We Cry for Our Son

We cry
The loss of our children,
Not just to others
But to their own madness,
The whirlwinds that swirled
And grew within them.

A mother lights candles
And says novenas
For her rebellious
Then prodigal son
Who returns home
One day
In a big fancy black car,
Dressed in a dark city suit
With a yellow flower pinned to his lapel.
He has become the feared killer
Of hated Don Novellino.

The father stays up
In his remote mountain-top garden
Until daylight's shame melts
Into evening shadows
And he has hoed his mind fine,
Beating clods and knots of thought.
What is this fate, the will of God,
The victory of a demon
That appeared one day
In his mouth
And defied the discipline of the field?

Better cold soup
Than to sit
On a bench
In the gloom of a kitchen
Whose mother's prayers
Go unheeded,
Whose bread
Is angrily kneaded.

Inside Etna

I do not conjure the reds and purples of Sicily's soft sunsets
Or tell of this centering isle of many greens,
Its gentle mountains,
Village-capped buttes,
Or rolling garden and rolling breasts of hill fields
And the lush flattened thighs
Of river valleys
On their curving descent to coastal lands
Where dinosaurs once trod and flew
And mosquitoes swarmed
And malaria recently ruled.

Rather, following the upper rim—
The great stone navel of Etna—
I seek to compass
The inner depths
Of a breathing and living mount
Pregnant
With molten lava.

However, with no prodding Virgil of my own,
I fear following Dante's path
Into this perilous inverted mortal cone
To make a descending journey
Into sins' darkening rounds
Where black rock runs in fiery red rivers,
Air bites acid,
Sulfur chokes,
And, suddenly,
The great explosion
And the fiendish festival
Of raining ash and ember.

My portholes into this world
Are tunnels, holes, chasms, crevices, caves, and collapses,
Sinkholes, mudslides, avalanches, earthquakes.
Or to let Italian vowels avalanche and tumble,
Buchi, crepe, voragini, crolli, dolini, frane, valanghe, terremoti
Tell of the Hades of our inner earth.

So I quake and shudder
Before lakes that boil
And freeze—
Where three men, in loveless ice's lake,
Relieve their pain
By gnawing on each other's heads.

The Glove of the Falconer

1

Anticipating release,
The hooded falcon nervously
Grips and re-grips the glove,
Spreads and closes the fan of its stiff feathers.

Cap off,
Swoosh:
He is gone
Into the thickening mist.

Blind
To the whirling gyre,
Beyond the call of whistle,
Peregrine, prodigal,
You now belong to the skies.

2

With the falcon
I fly my hope:
May Christ,
Crucified on skull hill
On knotted cross,
At the great divide
Of first and second creations
Call you home
From eye's journeying stars
And heart's nesting wounds.

Why I Write of Sicily

If I could take back from time
What God so generously gave
In flesh and form,
And time stole back
Through accident,
Disease,
Chaos and death,
I would have life,
Given in freshness and love,
Be my daily Eucharist
And grace-given memory
The evening chalice of the morrow's hope.

PART THREE

Essay

NUNNA ROSALIA

*In contrast to parents, with whom our relations may have been
too intense and immediate, grandparents, or perhaps a surrogate
great-uncle or aunt, prove the more easy gateway to the past and the
point from which to begin our research and thought on family histo-
ry. They could be our first and intimate contact with a distant past
that no longer exists in flesh, mind, and environment. The rich stuff
of past and memory, grandparents straddled past and present.
Grandparents were the children of the great- and great-great-
grandparents, whose individual traits, unless preserved in memoirs
and history books as they were by only a small portion of the literate
few, have been erased by forgetfulness or assumed into the body of
deep time by archetypes and myths of the family's beginning, origins
in strange lands, fantasies of static villages, tales of first migrations
and original settlements. The childhoods and youth of our grand-
parents belong to lost times and perennial, thus, frozen images. The
gulf and rupture of great events, mutations of cultures, transfor-
mations of society separate them from us. All the variations of fami-
ly, body, habit, gesture, emotion, and mind brought by successive
ages and epochs mark us off from them, making us different genera-
tions, and, so to speak, familiar strangers. Indeed, you must gather
and rethink grandparents and their stories. You must scour your
memory and family's to collect all their sayings, gestures, attitudes,
and intentions and give the coherence in their personalities and ex-
perience. And you must find and join in your history all possible
church and civil records, photographs, letters, newspapers, local his-
tories, scholarly books, and artifacts of every sort, including tools for*

carpentry and artifacts from sewing and other handcrafts. Yet, doing all of that does not cancel the more elemental fact that you knew them with the directness and the fullness of your fresh senses and impressionable and absorbing minds. You heard them with your parents, uncles and aunts, and other grandchildren. You were with them in body and spirit, in private and public, and in everyday ordinary things and exceptional events. You experienced the interior of their homes. You were with them when they made their way, perhaps for the first time ever or regularly, into a restaurant, danced at a wedding, or with difficulty walked the uneven ground and narrow lanes of family graves. You cuddled close to them, assumed their distinct body smells, and became accustomed to their peculiarly hesitant pattern of breathing. You adjusted your gait to their walk, knelt with them in bedtime prayers, and suffered their frustrations as they cried, lashed out, and even in the end lost control of their bladders and minds. Teaching you over decades the limits and ends of this mortal flesh, they taught you how to play cards, tell jokes, make a sling shot, walk on stilts, collect berries, bake a pie, or do a dozen other things that the contemporary world has forgotten how to do. In what they said, did, and experienced, grandparents belonged to different times and ways. They are the contrasting lives we knew intimately. With them we were as close to the distant past as we would ever be. Close to the core of memory, source of early impressions and senses, they are the living material amidst which we seek a self, define a family, and even fashion a tradition. In calling forth and entertaining our grandparents' lives and minds we become earnest about the past and the way in which it is us and we are it.

Of my four grandparents—my mother's father, William Linsdau, of Prussian and Irish ancestry; my mother's mother, Frances Boodry, of Acadian and English background; my father's father, Antonino Amato, who died as a young man ten years after his arrival

*from a village in the Madonie Mountains of northwest Sicily; and
my father's mother, Rosalia Notaro, Antonino's young bride from
his homeland—I address here Nunna Rosalia and her fate in Ameri-
ca.*

Rosalia, A Misery as Ancient as Sicily

The ethnicity we claim, either reflexively or by conscious choice,
provides us an identity, a past, and an inheritance. It can command
and distort our writing of family history. We must take care lest we
ignore details and subscribe to false truths in exchange for making
ourselves servants of contemporary ideologies. Selves and families
are not frozen entities that can be identified and preserved by attach-
ing to them words, names, and fashionable ideas. We must wear our
proclaimed selves and past lightly. Our exploration and imagination
must ever be active in honoring them with truths for which we've
labored.

My father, who liked grand arias, especially as sung by Caruso,
was an Italian who couldn't sing a note. Neither could I, who was
branded a listener early on in the third grade by a music teacher
who had a bad temper and strong dislike of me. Sicilian (not Ital-
ian), the only language my father spoke before going to school, was
never used in our home and was reserved for special times, particu-
larly emotional times, in my grandmother Rosalia's home. Our fam-
ily knew nothing of Italian high culture or the glories of Rome and
did nothing to assimilate this Italian inheritance. We were without
any relation to and even an iota of knowledge about the *Mafia*. Our
Cosa Nostra was food, jobs, a house, a car, making it through the
Depression, serving in World War II, in effect, taking care of our
own business. Living on the east side of Detroit, we were peasants
and new immigrants huddling under the shadow of Chrysler Mo-
tors. This was the neighborhood, the world we principally cared

about—and we forsook the places and ways of the mountain towns of Sicily that grandparents Rosalia and Antonino left behind.

Our name Amato—"the loved one"—announced and identified us as Italians to the outside world, which we met mainly at work, school, and in our mixed ethnic neighborhood of Germans, Irish, Canadians, and older Americans.[1] The two "a's"—one at the beginning and the other in the middle of our name—and the "o" marked us as Italian to outsiders, while making it seem right that relatives with such vowel-studded names as Messina, Rizzuto, Perna, Salamagna, and DeCarlo belonged properly with us as did our champions, to mention those my dad frequently referred to: Rocky Marciano, Joe DiMaggio, Mario Lanza, and Gugliemo Marconi. Stereotypes about us as Italians multiplied several fold with the revelation that we were Sicilian. But my family had their own lives and affairs to attend to, and they even excused and found humorous the occasional attempts by cousins to disown their Italian identity, as Cousin Steve did in pursuit of a blond at a family picnic. They had more to do in this world than to take insults and prejudices to heart. We were confident that we were more or less like every other working class group on the east side of Detroit—simply trying to make our own way in a changing society. Even though some of our relatives looked like tan and dark-eyed Arabs rather than fair Normans (as my grandmother, father, and his sisters did), and liked their olive oil, wine, and oregano, we were not black. And stereotyping and exclusion, however low grade but real they were, hadn't prevented my dad and uncles (the males in my immediate family) from successfully marrying Irish and German girls, being hired at work, and being drafted by the army.

---

[1] The name Amato is common in parts of Sicily and southern Italy and, thanks to emigration, can be found throughout Europe, Latin America, the United States, and elsewhere. It is also a name used by Spanish or Mediterranean Jews.

In my childhood, I can remember only once an angry friend's shouting *Dago* at me in front of a group, which mispronunciation of the Spanish name *Diego* with a single blow classified me as a separate and repulsive race. It awoke a stronger feeling than the mild taunting query that I suffered in elementary school come each Saint Patrick's Day. "Amato—that's Italian right?—what are you doing wearing green today?" I, usually of quick retort, was left speechlessly defenseless before this question since I couldn't say my mother made me wear green and celebrate Saint Patrick's Day. How was I, only a boy, to understand or give an account why Irish was the preferred ethnicity of mixed-breed Ethel Mary Linsdau Amato, who called herself Ethel May Linsdeau, to show her affection for her aunt and somehow to make herself Irish or French, anything other than the nationally despised German?

However, starting at university I began to examine my relation to Rosalia and my Italian-Sicilian-American identity, which I preferred over others in my heritage. First, being Italian was a way to be European; and this had the singular advantage of keeping me from being defined by what I took to be mass, materialistic, superficial, capitalist American society, which I—with little appreciation of what the nation had meant for my immigrant family and for me in particular—found repulsive. I disowned it in as many ways as scores of intellectuals and artists for more than a century had denounced the middle class, bourgeois society that birthed, educated, and nurtured them. In turn, with marriage and my own family, claiming Italian and Sicilian ancestry became a way to enter into community with my Carpatho-Russian wife's family and Polish and other friends, whose families were recent immigrants to the United States and children of the working classes.

In mid life, as I overtly rejected most ethnic identities as politically and even racially motivated and as self-adornment and snobbery for second and third generation immigrants, I used my tie to Rosalia to give my family and myself an identity with poor rural people and, above all, peasants, to whom I gravitated in my studies of France, Russia, and southern Italy, *il Mezzogiorno*. Affiliating with peasants connected me simultaneously to the deepest history and all rural peoples. More than membership in a prosaic political party or identity with endless loquacious left-wing causes or high-brow intellectual movements, peasants by universality, eccentricity, and anarchic disposition were a breed to my temperament and liking. Furthermore, they fit with living in southwestern rural Minnesota and my role as a teacher in the university's rural and regional studies program. Peasants lived locally and thought concretely; their truth was found in their proverbs and contradictions. They knew what fed them, who worked and who didn't, and whose manure pile was whose manure pile. Again to my liking, while conforming to my understanding of Rosalia and the preceding generations of relatives, peasants could be considered the victims and the enemies of abstract ideas and institutions, which were bent on making them the docile servants of market, nation, church, and party. I reveled in their concern for details and their embrace of single and seemingly contradictory truths about life, and I even lent my sympathies to justifying their harsh materialism, exclusive attachment to the family, skepticism about human motives, and the blending of religion and superstition into an attitude. Literature by a range of Sicilian, Italian, and European writers, such as Sicilian Giuseppe Verga, Ignazio Silone, and French rural writers Emile Guillaumin and Pierre-Jakez Hélas, broadened my imagination of and deepened my attachment to nineteenth- and twentieth-century peasantry. Supplemented by study of their history, I increasingly located the peasantry's plight at the heart of the modern world's transformation from rural to urban and naturally identified it with the conditions of my Sicilian immigrant family and the fate of my Rosalia.

My search for Rosalia led me further. It encouraged my study of Italian, the thriving historical field of European peasantry and rural life, and classic and contemporary histories of Sicily and southern Italy, which, collectively known as the *Mezzogiorno*, is defined as poor, rural, and agricultural regions that continued their decline since Italian unification and industrialization. My concern for social justice in contemporary life took me twice to western Sicily to visit and write on the influential non-violent social reformer of Partinico and Trappeto, Danilo Dolci. Receiving attention in American liberal circles, Dolci and his small team put several problems at the center of their analysis and made them targets for their reform: unemployment; the distribution of water; the condition of earthquake victims in the Bellice Valley; pervasive Mafia control and influence over the island's economic and political life; and the populace's traditional and fatalistic attitudes about their power over their own future.[2] I was left with no doubt that the interconnection of rural poverty and emigration in Sicily formed the core of my family's experience and accounted for their move to America. As I wrote in my poem "Dancing with My Grandparents" my ancestral family was "Without a donkey to mortgage, / A garden for tillage."

In the last fifteen years, pursuing my mounting interest in family history, I have gone to Sicily several times to establish and renew my acquaintance with the villages and families of Rosalia and Antonino and their ancestors. It has been exhilarating to cross an ocean and,

---

[2] For an introduction to Danilo Dolci and his work in Sicily, see his *Inchiesta à Palermo* (Torino: Einaudi, 1957), *Sicilian Lives* (New York: Pantheon, 1981), Joseph Amato, "Danilo Dolci: A Nonviolent Reformer in Sicily," eds. Severyn T. Bruyn and Paula M. Rayman, *Nonviolent Action and Social Change* (New York: Irvington Publishers, 1979), 165–85, and for a collection of testimonials, essays, and other writings on him, see http://danilo1970.interfree.it/dolci.html.

one hundred years since my grandparents' crossing, receive such a warm welcome from a lively and humble family who resemble in speech, generosity, emotion, and food the family I remember from my childhood.

In the last few years, with time swiftly catching up on me and feeling that I am the last keeper and caretaker of Rosalia's and the family's memory, I take it to be my job to keep the hearth. As I wrote in the last verse of a poem to a favorite uncle, my mother's brother, who kept his dead buddy afloat a whole night in a North African bay after their ship had been sunk by a German sub in the fall of 1942:

> And now, a half-century later,
> What seems a flood of time ago
> Since the trip of reclamation
> [to get Uncle Bill and his family in Boston and return them to Detroit],
> With my beloved grandparents Bill and Frances long gone,
> And my very own parents, Joe and Ethel,
> And even Bill and Margaret dead,
> I keep them,
> Together and afloat,
> In the dispersing seas of time.
> I do this
> With the buoying grace of memory
> And the treading kick of word and story.[3]

I take to heart the themes of Sicilian writer Giuseppe di Lampedusa's melancholy *Leopard*. Writing of the Sicily just joined to the mainland with the reunification that resulted from the Risorgi-

---

[3] Joseph Amato, "A Buddy Afloat," *Buoyancies: A Ballast Master's Log* (Marshall, MN/Granite Falls, MN: Crossings Press/Spoon River Poetry Press, 2014), 135.

mento, the perennial prize and cherished garden of the Mediterranean, which lured more than twenty civilizations and peoples to occupy it, Lampedusa contends that it cannot be reformed or yet rejuvenate itself. With the most ancient law of the stars and intractable givens of human nature, it daily sentences past and present alike to oblivion. In this most ancient of places, neither memory of yesterday or truth of today survive. "Nowhere," Lampedusa writes, "has truth so short a life as in Sicily; a fact scarcely happened five minutes before its genuine kernel has vanished, been camouflaged, embellished, disfigured, annihilated by imagination and before self-interest, shame, fear, generosity, malice, opportunism, charity, all the passions, good as well as evil, fling themselves on the fact and tear it to pieces; very soon its has vanished altogether." The dying prince grasps that he is the last of the aristocratic Salina line. As if to pull even memory down into the grave with him, his last reflections are "that a noble family lies entirely in its traditions, that is, its vital memories, and he was the last to have any unusual memories, anything different from those of other families." Many practitioners of genealogy and family history might secretly agree with me that this is true of every family. Of all those who occupy themselves with the past and the connection of generations, who does not, in fact, carry the ripening sorrow that death not only undoes the body and the tie to family but all testimonies, secrets, and experiences that life and family have revealed with them?

Approaching the serious age of seventy-seven, and the only son of Rosalia's only son, I look into the jaws of time, the open mouths of the Jurassic sharks that swam off young Sicily's shores. I ponder the line of Rosalia and Antonino a hundred years after they left Sicily for the United States, and almost twenty years after my father died. I ask myself if I am the last who will ever retrace their trail down from the hills of that ancient and testing island across a sea to this fresh and raw outpost of civilization called America and testify to the fact that, try as they could and did, they did not escape the labyrinth of poverty and the maze of suffering and death. I narrate my commemoration of them.

THE SICILY LEFT BEHIND

Rosalia, to whom I was so close as a grandson and whom I describe in detail at the end of this essay, was the umbilical cord that tied me to Europe, Italy, Sicily, yet to a small agricultural town in the Madonie Mountains above Palermo. Mother of my father, his sister and three stepsisters, a short and stocky widow dressed in black as long as I can remember and unfaltering in her affection for my father and me, Rosalia Notaro Amato was the vessel through which I sought myself in the past and tried to create an inheritance to combat the alien present of others' making. Doing what historians of their families commonly do with regard to their grandparents, at every point I scrutinized her ways, her passions, her cooking, her home, her goods, her garden, her beloved trips to the Italian store, and her fate for traces of an older and enduring tradition. She was a gyre of flesh calling me home to my deepest childhood and youthful days that so imprinted my mind and yet, center of my study, she flew me toward fertile and stony, rich and poor Sicily.

Rosalia's and Antonino's great crossing was anything but theirs alone. It belonged to an era and to one of the greatest movements of peoples in all of history. Their emigration cannot be conceived independent of the unprecedented exodus of Italians and Europeans to the New World in the last decades of the nineteenth century and at the start of the twentieth. While lives and stories are not to be denied individuality and heroism, my grandparents, like participants in war or any other common act of this era of centralized state and world markets, are to be quantified along with millions of others.

146

They, who count so much to me, tally only two of the 3.5 million Italians who left home for the New World between 1901 and 1910; only two of the 7 million who emigrated to the New World between 1871 and 1914. Part of the great transfusion of America with European peoples and cultures and types, they are the smallest unit of the 30 million European immigrants who arrived in the United States between 1870 and 1914. Their epochal journey belongs to a greater narrative: that immense, dramatic, and accelerating upheaval of population that occurred in the last decades of the nineteenth century as the phenomenal expansion of cheap steamship and railroad travel, in combination with the most precious (because most basic) promises of work and money, scoured the most remote corners of southern and eastern Europe for immigrants to work in mines, forests, and the booming factories of the United States and Canada, and to settle the towns and inner reaches of Brazil and Argentina.[4]

Their stories belong to yet another narrative. By birth and condition Rosalia and Antonino belonged to the plight of landless poor, as did at some point the ancestry of the Linsdau and Boodry and other families who comprised my background. Rosalia and Antonino were members of Europe's largest family, the peasantry, which as a class has been on the edge of need since European feudalism, the Catholic Church, and the emerging trans-regional markets formed them into a class around the year 1000.[5] I found that I cannot read the rich history of European peasantry, in all their variation

---

[4] Walter Nugent, *Crossings: The Great Transatlantic Migrations, 1870–1914* (Bloomington: Indiana University Press, 1992), xii–xiii, 11–14. See also, for Italian emigration, ed. Gianfusto Rosoli, *Un Secolo di Emigrazione Italiana, 1876–1976* (Roma: Centro Studi Emigrazione, 1978).

[5] Central for the formation of the European peasant is David Levine, *At the Dawn of Modernity: Biology, Culture, and Material Life* (Berkeley: University of California Press, 2001), 43–44, 192–195, 208–209, passim.

of location and time, without harvesting insights or compounding questions I have about the lives of Rosalia and Antonino.[6]

I know for sure that they were not the peasants who, in the words of Romantic historian Jules Michelet, "loved only the land. That is the sum of their religion! They worship only the manure on their fields."[7] Rather, my grandparents in Sicily, a land exploding in population for a hundred years, were extra children on an island awash in surplus humans; it had once exported wheat and animal products to the world and would begin to export its children.[8] If they and the family clung to the hope of ever having a place on the land, it was because, until the promise of emigration appeared, it was the only hope they knew and could imagine. The smallest gardens were the only rafts they had, even though they floated them into a sea of vicissitudes—droughts, mudslides, crop failures, and plagues. Land assured all of a lifetime of hard work and inevitably brought bitter harvests of scarcity and misery. And what little land they owned or worked didn't insulate them against inferiority, insults, and shame, not be forgotten or avenged. It left few doubts that God's bounty lay elsewhere. Steadfastness and resignation drawing short of despair were the only answer.

The land also subjected its servants and aspirants to man-made calamities, which were never lacking in colonized and administered

---

[6] A few works of interest on the peasantry are Emmanuel LeRoy Ladurie, *Montaillou: The Promised Land of Error* (New York: Random House, 1979), Piero Camporesi, *Il pane selvaggio* (Bologna: Mulino, 1983), Carlo Ginzburg, *The Cheese and the Worms* (Baltimore, MD: Johns Hopkins University Press, 1980), and Arthur Imhof, *Lost Worlds: How Our European Ancestors Coped with Everyday Life and Why Life Is So Hard Today* (Charlottesville: University of Virginia Press, 1996).

[7] Cited in Joseph Amato, *Servants of the Land: God, Family, and Farm, The Trinity of Belgian Economic Folkways in Southwestern Minnesota* (Marshall, MN: Crossings Press, 1990), 57.

[8] Jane Schneider and Peter Schneider, *Culture and Political Economy in Western Sicily* (New York: Academic Press, 1976), IX–X.

Sicily. They came incarnate as tax collectors, stewards of the absentee lord's land, local attorneys and officials, along with packs of shrewd and swindling merchants, dishonest bankers, greedy priests, ambitious politicians, and Mafia, the controlling agents of absentee landlords.

With a need not dissimilar to that of my nineteenth-century relatives from the swamps of Acadia, the overpopulated Irish and English countryside, and the rocky and parsimonious lands of Maine and western New York, my Sicilian grandparents suffered the common plight of the rural poor everywhere. They did not have a secure niche on the land. They were without money, overtaxed, too populous, and were driven to migrate if they were to marry, to have something, and to be somebody. Whether classified peasants or rural poor, Rosalia and Antonino belonged to a class, a place, and a time in which the poor were in motion, both under the spell of the most traditional values, in the grasp of capitalism, and in the process of organizing and even revolting, anything but "potatoes in a sack."[9]

Their homes were in nearby agro-hill towns of Montemaggiore and Cerda along the River Torto. Hundreds of feet above the sea and to the south of the port town Termine Imerese, one bay away to the east from Palermo, these towns enjoyed *aria fresca* and were upland refuges from malaria (*mal aria*), which had ravaged the Italian seaside lands since Roman times until two or three generations ago. Without good roads or animals and carts to haul them, the towns'

[9] For this quotation and two books on the transformation of the countryside and its people in late nineteenth-century western Sicily, see Donna Rae Gabaccia, *Militants and Migrants: Rural Sicilians Become American Workers* (New Brunswick, NJ: Rutgers University Press, 1988), 7, and esp. 1–36, and *From Sicily to Elizabeth Street: Housing and Social Change Among Italian Immigrants, 1880–1930* (Albany: State University of New York Press, 1984.) Also, for a worthy examination of economic conditions in western Sicily precipitating migration to the United States, see Virginia Yans-McLaughlin, *Family and Community: Italian Immigrants in Buffalo, 1880–1930* (Ithaca, NY: Cornell University Press, 1977).

poor were isolated. It is unlikely that Rosalia and Antonino ever traveled far before their great emigration. They probably never visited nearby seaside Cefalù, where medieval Norman king Roger II built his great cathedral, or visited Palermo, at one point medieval Europe's largest city. Like most peasants and rural poor they were essentially tethered to the place from which they traveled between sun up and sun down.

Insofar as need and necessity left them room for an identity, it was local and particular. They were known by their place in the family and their family's condition, whether it had land, a good garden, a mule or donkey, decent friends and godfathers, who formed a vital system of support and protection, and yet a decent landlord who stuck with them in bad times. In mountain towns, like Cerda and Montemaggiore, they were identified by which end of town they exited and toward what field they traveled. The more prosperous workers left to cultivate and then harvest their own fields, gardens, and olive trees, while the poorest—the gatherers, shepherds, and day laborers, including young Rosalia Notaro and her family—went out to work land owned by others, pick greens, or forage in forests.

Church and municipal records identify the Notaro family in Montemaggiore as early as 1750 and the Amatos in Cerda as early as 1815. The length of time a family spent in a particular town indicates persistence and at least minimal well being in a region in which micro-regional migrations, accelerating through much of rural Italy and Europe, were becoming increasingly necessary to find work and earn money. Certainly, migration, which was common to the European peasantry and poor since their formation in the Middle Ages, frustrates genealogists especially in their searches for poor, thus mobile, families and denies certainty to family historians who mistakenly seek singular origins in fixed and static villages and towns of Europe. In any case, as the nineteenth century unfolded in Sicily excess population and shortage of land, work, and wages converged to deny both the Notaro and Amato families both security and opportunity in their declining towns.

Both families inhabited the countryside and, though known by such common terms as *contadini, coltivatori,* and *compagnoli,* they were most commonly designated as *villici,* meaning landless or land-poor peasants who lived outside the village center and in remote communes near the fields they tended. Every August, the *villici* appeared before the local *gabellotti* (land agents) to seek a contract for the next growing season. Because the contract called for delivery of a specified amount of grain, the desperate *villici* constantly had to increase the promised yields in order to assure the rental of their land. This harsh arrangement forced the impoverished sharecroppers to exhaust the very land they tilled.[10]

If the Amatos owned a home, which our present-day family members in Cerda doubt, it probably consisted of a single room with an earthen floor. Furnishings would have been sparse—a table, a bench, perhaps a chair, a saint's statue, an oven or stove, a large bed for the parents, and a cradle, nearly continuously occupied. Children would have slept on straw mattresses, crowded together in a small loft. If they had more than a single room, animals surely would have shared it. They would have had a minimum of personal belongings—not much more than a religious relic, some sort of calendar, candles, a scrap of lace, a large table, a stool or two, some utensils for cooking, needles and thread for sewing and crocheting, and a small collection of tools, perhaps including tongs, shears, a shovel, a saw, an axe, and an adze.

A photograph of Antonino's father, Giuseppe, taken when he was in his late forties or early fifties, tells the toll life took on poor

---

[10] John W. Briggs, *An Italian Passage: Immigrants to Three American Cities, 1890-1930* (New Haven, CT: Yale University Press, 1978), 19-20.

Sicilian peasants in the late nineteenth century. A prominent nose, reminding me of my father's, forlorn eyes, and large ears, distinguish his thin, creased, and unshaven face. He wears a cravat around his scrawny neck, a tattered coat, a collarless shirt, and a worn vest missing one of its four buttons.

Poverty and subsistence farming dominate my family's history in Antonino's Cerda and Rosalia's Montemaggiore. With their towns increasingly serving as biological incubators for the richer valleys and prospering towns below and even beyond Sicily, my Sicilian grandparents' lives resembled those of mountain peasants and rural folks in modern times.[11] Like all mountain people who did not control rich valleys but who worked scanty, rocky, and cold uplands, my Italian relations resembled the great majority of peasants who lived in villages, cultivated the land, and became ever more entangled in an economic system of exploitation of the countryside that increasingly left peasants without land and even lands to rent and, further fueling downward mobility, turned them, agricultural laborers and small craftsmen, into day laborers, *giornalieri*, "who compos[ing] the bulk of south Italy's work force, fared worst of all."[12] Their fates were not their own. Like twigs taken by a mighty spring torrent, my grandparents were swept down, out of the mountains of Sicily, into the ocean and out to the wider world.

---

[11] For a classic portrait of the nineteenth-century Sicilian peasant, see Giuseppe Pitré's monumental *Biblioteca delle tradizioni popolari siciliane*, 25 vols., published between 1871 and 1913, which was compiled contemporaneously with the lives of young Antonino and Rosalia. Also, see Salvatore Salomone-Marino, *Customs and Habits of Sicilian Peasants* (London: Associated University Presses, 1981), Charlotte Gower Chapman, *Milocca: A Sicilian Village* (Cambridge, MA: Schenkman, 1971), and Cristoforo Grisanti, *Folklore di Isnello* (Palermo: Sellerio, 1981).

[12] For the economic conditions of Sicily, see Virginia Yans-McLaughlin, *Family and Community*, 25–34; for quotation of day laborers, see Yans-McLaughlin, 30.

Their descent, the downward trajectory of their class and family, began well before they were born. In the largest perspective, historical vectors spanning generations determined Antonino and Rosalia's need and choice to emigrate to the United States. In the course of three centuries, commercial agriculture dismantled traditional land-holding institutions. Outside money and the state altered the peasants' relation to the land and tromped local arrangements and traditional protections. Distant European markets came to dictate regional changes. Baronial hamlets became embryonic towns, and towns, especially those along the coasts, grew larger. (As early as 1652, Montemaggiore already had 1,200 inhabitants.) Coincidentally, absentee landlordism spread and estates fell under the management of hated middlemen, *gabellotti*. As cash increasingly determined transactions in the countryside, traditional contractual relationships, which once provided a measure of security, vanished. Landlords invited in outside laborers from Greece and Albania, which possibly accounts for the origins of Rosalia's maiden name, *Albanese*. In the course of these centuries and then with accelerated intensity in the nineteenth century, Rosalia and Antonino's ancestors, peasants by need and mentality, were metamorphosed into economic beings. Starting as early as the sixteenth century, Sicily, long a colony, was placed in the service of the emerging European grain market. During the next two centuries, the Sicilian interior increasingly fell under the control of the island's growing urban centers; and a new money class composed of bankers, landlords, tax collectors, and landlords in the service of exterior forces took hold of the island. Between 1798 and 1861, a period marked by Italian unification and coincident with a mounting crisis of the island's feudal structures, Sicily's population rose from 1.6 to 2.4 million, testifying to diminishing mortality rates. No longer concentrated in the upland grain lands, which travelers frequently see only as vast and empty expanses, the rural population steadily relocated to larger towns and along the coasts.

Natural elements and social forces interacted and intensified in the course of the nineteenth century, setting increasing numbers of the island's and southern Italy's population in local motion to towns and upon path of migration to distant lands. Forming diverse streams and chains, and divided between temporary and permanent, migration increasingly took on a regional, European, and a transatlantic character. Even with Italy's having the second largest emigration to the New World, its population, nevertheless, rose from 28 million in 1871 to 35 million in 1914.[13] In parallel fashion, despite massive emigration, Sicily's population grew from 1.5 million in 1800 to 3.5 million in 1900, with population density tripling in western Sicily. With as few as one in six peasants on this crowded landscape owning any land in Sicily, farm plots for those who did own land were too small to produce an increasingly necessary cash income and frequently too dispersed and far from home to consolidate a secure existence. Though these conditions were in play across Europe and North America, they reached such levels of intensity in Sicily that they metamorphosed peasants like those of Antonino's and Rosalia's families into seasonal and day laborers—poor without any tie to the land—and dramatically increased their migration in the second half of the century (Nugent, 96).

Peasants who still owned land lacked capital to invest in fertilizers and irrigation. Also absentee landlords—gentry, nobility, and church—did not invest in modernizing their lands (Nugent, 96). As known for a long time, only the central government could save Sicily. In addition to breaking up the *latifundia*—the large estates, especially on the western end of the island, which raised wheat in rotation with natural pastures—the government would have to transform

---

[13] Nugent, *Crossings*, 95.

the island's agriculture, society, and ecology. This would require re-foresting mountains, launching irrigation projects, building villages, hamlets, and roads, and planting diversified labor-intensive crops. But, alas, what the preceding regime, the Bourbons, would not pay for, the new government of Italian unification, 1860 to 1870, consciously chose not to do. Instead, it supported industrialization of the nation with adoption of policies supporting free trade and an open economy. The government's removal of protective trade barriers, and the re-imposition of a grist tax also worked against the locally based economies of Sicilian peasants and craftsmen (Nugent, 118-20).

Not without parallel to the effects of the open market on the rural poor across the entire world in the last few decades, Italy's entrance into European and world markets had the effect of squeezing the island's multiplying rural poor off the land, out of work, and into massive emigration. For western Sicily, the region of Rosalia and Antonino, this drama was intensified by a decline in the export of its principal crop, wheat, because of competition from Russian wheat and then expanding North and South American wheat production; and the mounting import of mass-produced goods displaced workers in indigenous crafts such as textile manufacture, candle- and tile-making, ceramics, hide-tanning, fish conservation, boat building, and coral polishing (Nugent, 114-15). Intensifying a further decline in local power and autonomy, swelling emigration coincided with the rise of the Mafia, which functioned as rural entrepreneurs who bridged gaps between the superstructure of government and outside markets on the one hand and local infrastructures and populations on the other.[14]

---

[14] Nugent, X, 9. Also, useful for the Sicilian Mafia is Anton Blok, *The Mafia of a Sicilian, 1860-1960* (New York: Harper and Row, 1974).

According to an 1886 Italian government report on agricultural conditions in the Sicilian countryside, the peasant class (*la classe dei contadini*) was miserable because its members often could not find enough agricultural work to provide an adequate living.[15] The frequency of poor harvests in this period worsened the deteriorating condition of the rural poor, who lacked cash to rent or buy land, to purchase essential goods, to defray the rising costs of services such as milling, or to pay the ever-increasing taxes remorselessly imposed by church and state. In this condition peasants, *villici*, found themselves forced to mortgage their homes and to sell their donkeys, mules, and homes to make it through the winter and prepare spring planting. Sharecroppers were thrown more and more on the mercy of the landholder or his agent; and some day laborers, living day to day, hand to mouth, lacked even the meager means to emigrate.[16] As this disastrous agricultural situation reached its nadir at the end of the century with an Italian-French trade war, Sicilian historian Giuseppe De Felice observed, "The little proprietors melt[ed] like the snow before the sun."[17] Among them were Antonino and Rosalia, whose journey to and lives in America began like millions of others in the historic transformation of the countryside and population of a continent, a nation, an island, and a region.

My paternal grandparents, along with their neighbors in the Madonie Mountains of Sicily, were being siphoned, more and more sucked, out of the hills of Sicily to form a flood of emigrants. To have work, earn money, have a mate, a family, and home of their

---

[15] *Inchiesta Jacini Atti della Giunta per Inchiesta agraria e sulle condizioni della classes agricole*, Vol. XIII (Rome, 1886), 667.
[16] Emilio Sereni, *History of the Italian Agricultural Landscape* (Princeton, NJ: Princeton University Press, 1997), 281–282, and Salvatore Francesco Romano, *Storia della Sicilia Post-Unificazione, Parte Seconda* (Palermo: Società *siciliana di Storia Patria*, 1958), 140–65.
[17] Briggs, *An Italian Passage*, 7.

own, the singularly desirable, respectable, and honorable thing to do increasingly equated to one command: leave, if you can. Forsaking the country and the land that provided neither food nor hope made emigration as much a necessity as a risk.

By 1900, on the threshold of the peak emigration and Antonino's and Rosalia's departures, Sicilians could be understood to have fully staged themselves for leaving. Approximately 70 percent of the Sicilian population lived in communities of ten thousand, which were concentrated at lower elevations and closer to the sea, where agricultural conditions were better, work was more available, and ships departing for the New World were at anchor.

Doing what Sicilian males had been doing in ever greater number as part of their migration strategy, Antonino set out alone to join waiting relatives in the New World. Once established there he would send for a bride, help bring family members, and reconstruct a village in which they were somebody. In 1904, Antonino joined thirty thousand other of his countrymen in emigrating. Two years later in 1906 Rosalia emigrated with one hundred twenty-eight thousand other Sicilians. In that year, eight hundred thousand Italians departed for foreign lands, three hundred seventy thousand of whom went to North America.

Antonino and Rosalia did not know how to envision their future in the New World. They had no assurance that *la miseria*, the companion of the Sicilian poor, would not follow them to the New World. But they had every reason to guess that things were not going improve for them and their kind in Sicily, whose riches, history, and power belonged to others. On this count, they were right. Amato family photographs from the next half-century suggest that things improved but not greatly. One photo taken before the Second World War, when Mussolini drove the Mafia from the island, testifies to their humble conditions having improved. One taken some twenty years later, after the war, shows the family of Antonino's sister Francesca. Gathered around her stands a husband and nine children in front of a modest home in need of repair. However, dressed in their Sunday best, we see everyone in the picture is clean, well groomed, and wearing shoes.

The last three letters our American family received from Cerda came after the Second World War, between 1949 and 1951. In them Francesca, writing to her sister Margherita in Detroit, expressed gratitude for the modest sums of money our family had provided, hoped for a package of clothes, and sent prayers, greetings, and wishes for Rosalia with condolences for her son-in-law. A second letter lists penny for penny all the ingredients bought to prepare *un tavola di San Giuseppe*, a modest dinner without meat served to neighbors and their children to honor Saint Joseph and seek his help in curing Margherita's son, Sam. Witnessing the wolf still at the family door, the third letter reports that simultaneously the town doctor and butcher are suing the family for unpaid bills and that the family waits for the outcome of a judicial hearing to determine whom they should pay first.

Almost a half century after Antonino left Sicily his family remained poor and in place. Only around 1950 did Antonino's sister and her husband acquire the family's first garden and olive tree, which have continued to supply them with food and oil and a little cash to this day. (Indeed, fifteen years ago, at the table of Antonino's grandniece Francesca and her husband Francesco, I was told how they remained with barely a penny to their name and no property until after World War II. Later in the day, Francesco told me how he, a son of a large family of sharecroppers who lived in a house provided by the patron, acquired their small garden of an acre, the very one in which we sat, by gathering and selling as scrap the shell cases that Patton's army expended and left behind on its drive down

158

the mountains to Palermo.) A few lines from "Francesco's Garden,"
a poem in this volume, says:

> With the money earned from scrap iron,
> Francesco bought a small garden.
> He made it a green raft
> Of beans, artichokes, and tomatoes,
> On which he floated wife Francesca
> And seven children
> To a new century.

ANTONINO'S STORY

Nunnu Antonino never completed his journey to old age, to the
luxury of retirement and a porch on which he would tell me, the
only son of his only surviving son, how things were in the old coun-
try, how he struggled there without luck to have something, anything
he could call his own. Antonino died when my father was not yet
three, before my father could form a memory of him, let alone learn
of his youth or the past. The cheap black metal crucifix I possess,
taken from inside his casket before they buried him, which passed
from Rosalia to my father and then me, seems unworthy of his
death and its consequences; yet, but a piece of mute and plain met-
al, it compassed the suffering that lay ahead for Rosalia and the fam-
ily.

His wedding photograph presents me with a short square-jawed
man, of even features and large shoulders, who without towering
over her yet diminishes his petite bride, 4' 7" Rosalia. A few surviv-
ing stories about him also give him some life in my mind, but they
do not succeed in making him as palpable and memorable as Rosa-
lia or my other two grandparents, whom I knew, as we know best, in
and through flesh for more than twenty years. My reason dissents
from the idea that his misfortune somehow secured the family bless-

159

ing in its continued crossing as migrants and immigrants. Emotional vines, the honeysuckle wrapped on the trunk of every family history, do not bring him to life. That rests on my historical creation of him.

I began by consulting relevant documents. His baptismal certificate records that Antonino was born in Cerda, Provincia Palermo, in 1881, to Giuseppe Amato and wife, Epifania Rizzo (of whom my father's sister Fina is the namesake). The April 1904 ship manifest for the *Marco Minghetti*, a slow ship of 12 knots service speed, lists third-class passenger Antonino as a workman who, significantly, could read and write. After a long voyage from Palermo, he arrived in New York City with $4 and a train ticket.[18] His next destination was the small northeastern Pennsylvania coal-mining town of Kelayres. There he would join his uncle Giuseppe Rizzo, who had reached the New World a year earlier. The risks of migration were somewhat offset by the promise of financial reward for unskilled workers like Antonino and Giuseppe. By working as so-called pick men in the coal mines, they might earn under the best conditions as much as $500 a year, which would be five or even ten times what they would make in Sicily, if they could find steady employment.

So many Sicilians settled in Kelayres that the town's Front Street resembled streets in Cerda and Montemaggiore. With such names as Sacco, McAloose, Villano, Capriotti, Nazzareno, Tornabene, Malatesta, Festa, Fiorci, Profetta, Aiello, DiMaria, and Jumpeter (Gian Pietro), its cemetery still reflects the type of chain migration that joined distant villages in Sicily to places in the New World. Located in Klein Township, one of the last township settlements plat-

---

[18] The Marco Minghetti, a slow ship of 12 knots service speed that would have taken weeks to clear the Mediterranean and cross the Atlantic, carried 960 passengers (24 first class, 936 third class) and would have cost between $15 and $25 for the trip from Palermo to New York, with Antonino responsible for feeding himself on route. This, I calculate, could have amounted to as much as a half-year or more of salary in Sicily.

ted in Schuylkill County in 1872, Kelayres was a patch town, a company settlement, named for early Irish residents Kelly and Ayres, who were construction supervisors for the Leigh Valley Railroad in the 1890s. Today, Kelayres, evoking its inseparable tie with coal mining, is shadowed on the north and east by high mounds of slag left over from open-pit mining conducted after the Second World War.

Two factors, among many, made it inevitable that, as an adult, I would frequently visit Kelayres, the town that welcomed my grandparents to America. It shares a border with my wife's hometown, McAdoo, a larger coal town to the east, which was incorporated into a borough in 1896; and my wife's father, Adam Bavolack, was burgess for more than a decade. Additionally, Kelayres was still filled with cousins, whom my grandmother and parents knew and I had even visited once as boy of eleven. In the 1970s I had several conversations with ninety-year-old retired local teacher Tony DiMaria, who not only knew many of the early Sicilian settlers of Kelayres but actually remembered our Antonino. Tony whetted my interest in learning about Kelayres, with the epochal but only regionally remembered 1934 Massacre, which is at the heart of "War of the Saints,"[19] and stories about the town's early Sicilian settlers, many of whom left Kelayres before World War I for industrial jobs in Buffalo, Rochester, and Detroit.[20] He recounted, for example, how one

---

[19] The Kelayres Massacre, though largely ignored by historians, arose out of intensifying local political struggle over patronage between the controlling Republican family, headed by Joseph Bruno, and the aspiring Democrats. The Bruno family, as tried and convicted, fired on the parading protesters on the eve of the election, killing six and wounding twelve of them.

[20] A useful study of contemporary Sicilian immigration to and settlement in Buffalo, New York, which lists Montemaggiore Belsito, and such neighboring communities as Cefalù, Valledolmo, Caltavuturo, Bagheria, Termini Imerese, and others, is Yans-McLaughlin, *Family and Community*. Also, useful for early Sicilian and Italian community are Jerre Mangione's memoir of Sicilian settlement in Roches-

161

Italian immigrant in Kelayres dealt with the nuisance of Irish-immigrant baseball players chasing pop flies into his garden. He retrieved from his dresser a pistol he had brought with him from the old country, returned to his garden patch and shot both the catcher and the pitcher in the leg. "No authorities came and arrested the Italian, and the Irish thereafter quit chasing pop-ups in his zucchini," Tony concluded.

Unfortunately, Tony could not offer even a physical description of my grandfather. He was able to confirm only that Antonino had worked in a local grocery store for a while. Although he wanted to earn a miner's wage—then about $1.25 a day—he knew after only one day that he would never descend into the blackness of a mine again. Surely, he could not have received more than a dollar a day clerking at the grocery.

Except for that single framed wedding photograph of him that stood among the candles, crocheted doilies, and a ceramic statuette of the Infant of Prague, which as ensemble formed a kind of shrine atop my grandmother's bedroom dresser, Antonino morphs into the general form of all those poor Sicilian peasants who would never get those few sustaining acres on which to cultivate some vines, an olive tree, a few rows of artichokes, eggplants, ceci beans, melons, and a few chickens; who never owned the nobleman's horse, the landowner's mule, but only a donkey, which was frequently mortgaged for seed money. He simply was one of the many who were driven from their homeland by a succession of bad crops, greedy

ter, New York, *Mount Allegro* (New York: Columbia University Press, 1981); Donna Gabaccia, *From Sicily to Elizabeth Street* (Albany: State University of New York, 1984), the exuberant spoken autobiography *Rosa, The Life of an Italian Immigrant,* written down by Marie Hall Ets (Minneapolis: University of Minnesota Press, 1970), and Rudolph Vecoli's seminal critique of Oscar Handlin's failure to recognize continuities and communities among immigrants, "Contadini in Chicago: A Critque of *The Uprooted," Journal of American History* 51 (1964–65), 404–417.

lords, indifferent government, high taxes, and all the other exploiters and parasites, who took what little money they had. Surely he heard and considered the cautionary Italian proverb: "He who leaves the old way for the new knows what he is losing but not what he will find." But he found a more convincing truth in the peasant proverb, "He who hasn't, isn't." Across the sea and up the mountains, he heard a beckoning voice of inviting relatives promising the chance in America to have something.

The twenty-three-year-old Antonino, who arrived in Kelayres in 1904, came, as Rosalia did, as part of a chain migration of family, village, and region. Coming with the help of his maternal uncle, he in his turn assisted the immigration of two of his younger sisters, my great-aunts Margherita and Carmela in 1909 and 1912 respectively. Suggesting that neighbors marry neighbors, he took up residence in Kelayres near Rosalia's older brother Pietro Notaro, who had arrived a few years before from Montemaggiore Belsito, a town just a few miles up the mountain from Cerda. Pietro's younger brother Cruciano, who married Antonino's sister Margherita, followed in 1902. Cruciano came to Kelayres with great-uncle Joe DeCarlo, who came two years before Rosalia's older sister Pauline, whom he had married and left behind pregnant. His intent, that of almost every poor immigrant young man who intended to stay rather than the 50 percent who returned at the end of their first year, was to have a wife, a family, and a village in this new land.[21]

ROSALIA, *LA DESTINATA*

Nunna Rosalia, my Sicilian paternal grandmother, led a fated life, one she neither chose nor planned. She simply had a destiny. Choice was not her rudder; books and dreams were not her sails; and ambitions did not transport her. Instead, family, that enduring

---

[21] Klaus J. Bade, *Migration in European History* (Oxford: Blackwell, 2003*)*, 113.

vessel, was her ship; and her companion was a misery as old as Sicily, a misery so openly keened in the Old World and so real but unrecognized in the New World, a misery that, along with so much else, put my grandmother and her home in contradiction to the progressing America in which we were enrolling.

In 1906, at age nineteen, Rosalia left Sicily never to return. Rosalia offered glimpses into her past. Once she told me that she encountered a big black snake in an olive orchard. Although she was proud of her schooling, she attended school for only two years before being sent to the fields to work, where she received two crusts of bread for a day of gleaning a farmer's field on a distant hillside. On our autumn trips through southern Michigan, she declared that our rich fruit harvest was inferior to those of verdant and fertile Sicily, never explaining why she did not share in its bounty or have the slightest wish to return to her *bel paese*. However, she once related an anecdote that revealed the answer to both these questions. One day, the local prince threw coins from his carriage, and she and her companions—greedily, "like chickens"—rushed and scraped to gather them up from between the cobblestones. The proverb about her mountain hometown, "*Muntimajurisi, mangiaghiènnari*" (the people from Montemaggiore eat acorns), suggests the scarcity of the country that failed to nurture Rosalia and accounts for why she left her *paese* for America.

With the young husbands and men leaving first for the New World, few women traveled and settled in America. Mores forbade young women who were not the heads of families to travel without husbands or chaperones or yet to work in the houses of others. A song of the era, recorded in Roseto, Pennsylvania (a well studied Italian immigrant community), reveals the dilemma of the young woman determined to have a man and family. She calls out and her mother responds:

164

Mother, mother, give me a hundred lire
For to America I want to go,
I won't give you the hundred lire.
And to America, no, no, no!

If you don't let me go to America
Out of the window I shall jump.
I won't let you go to America.
Better dead than dishonored.[22]

Rosalia went with two brothers waiting for her. Yet, hope as she did, she did not leave the world of *la miseria* behind. She married on the basis of an exchange of photographs. On mutual examination, she took Antonino to be a handsome and solid man from her region, a village only five miles down the mountain, and he took Rosalia to be a fitting bride and would bring her to Kelayres, where he worked and where she would find other *paesani* and her older brother Pietro, with whom she lived until married and who may have been the architect of the marriage. The 1906 manifest for the ship *Lazio* recorded Rosalia as being a nineteen-year-old "workwoman." Like Antonino, she arrived with $4 to her name. Her indicated destination was the home of her younger brother Cruciano, who lived in the town of Hazelton, a few miles to the north of Kelayres. Rosalia and Antonino wed the following spring, in 1907, about six months after Rosalia's arrival.

Unable to find satisfactory work in and around Kelayres since the day he surfaced from the mines for the first time and determined never to descend again, Antonino—with Rosalia and their infant son,

[22] Folk song "Mother Give Me a Hundred Lire," transcribed by Carla Bianco in Roseto, Pennslyvania, *The Two Rosetos* (Bloomington: University of Indiana Press, 1974), 37.

Joseph, named after and thus linked to his paternal grandfather—moved to Detroit in 1911. The promise of better-paying factory jobs in the burgeoning auto industry made their destination the new century's fastest-growing American city. In 1913, the year Henry Ford introduced the revolutionizing assembly line in his Highland Park plant in metro Detroit and a year before he offered to pay all of his workers $5 dollars a day, basic daily pay for a laborer was $2.34, or 26 cents an hour. These wages made city work significantly better than country work, in light of the fact that a farm hand earned only a dollar a day and a mill worker $1.25 and an urban family lived on $10 a week, with a five-room downstairs flat renting for only $14 a month and a man's overcoat costing $10.[23]

In choosing to go to Detroit, which had 285,000 inhabitants in 1900 and 466,000 in 1910 and received more immigrants between 1900 and 1920 than any other U.S. city except New York and Chicago, Antonino and Rosalia joined about ten thousand other Italians, who were employed by the city water works, the Michigan Central Railroad, the Pingree and Smith Shoe Factory, and various auto and stove manufacturers. Among them also were entrepreneurs who owned small stores, saloons, and produce stands.[24] The young couple settled on Russell Street in a downtown neighborhood whose residents were nearly all Italian, mostly from Sicily, Lombardy, and Genoa.[25]

---

[23] William Adams Simonds, *Henry Ford: His Life, His Work, His Genius* (New York: Bobbs-Merrill, 1943), 137.

[24] Vittorio Re, *The History of the First Presbyterian Church of Detroit* (Detroit, MI: Ethnic Studies Division, Center for Urban Studies, Wayne State University Press, 1979), 1.

[25] Not surprisingly, the host community didn't distinguish among the different regional origins of the new immigrants it classified as "obscure working folks," in the words of local historian Louis Rankin, "Detroit Nationality Groups," *Michigan History Magazine* 23 (Spring 1939), 163.

Antonino and Rosalia arrived late, as the poor usually do. They came amid the mini-depression of 1910–12. Antonino scoured the immense industrial landscape for work along with tens of thousands of others. On one occasion, he followed a rumor of available work at the new Ford plant in nearby Highland Park to join a large, unruly crowd that pushed against the fences. Plant security police drove the job seekers off the property by spraying them away with powerful fire hoses. Rosalia told how Antonino had returned home wet and dejected.

By 1915 Antonino and Rosalia were making headway in Detroit. He had obtained a day-laborer job at the Anderson Forge Company. They even had—you can imagine their joy—sufficient funds to buy a house on the east side's Beniteau Avenue, two miles from downtown, in a neighborhood where Italians and other immigrants bought their first cherished home, by which they measured the success or failure of subsequent immigrants, including homeless whites and blacks in the 1940s, 50s, and later. At home in an Italian and Sicilian community, they could speak their own tongue, buy familiar foods, and feel connected to the villages and family they left behind in Sicily and Pennsylvania.

In 1912, my father, Joseph, was born. Later a baby sister, Epifania (Fina), was born. The two scarcely compensated for the loss of an older brother, also named Joseph, who had suffered fatal burns shortly after their arrival in Detroit after accidentally overturning Rosalia's scrub bucket filled with scalding water on himself. Another tragedy soon followed. On a horrible October day in 1915, fate struck again and far harder. Antonino, only thirty-three years old, came home from work, complained of feeling sick, and collapsed into Rosalia's arms. He died the next morning from a burst appendix. Rosalia could have no doubt that *la miseria*, the companion and ever-present shadow of the Sicilian poor, had followed them across the sea through the Golden Gate of America. Rosalia, in an instant, was destined for an unhappy life. "The bad," an old proverb runs, "arrives on horseback and departs on foot." Not even thirty years old, young widow Rosalia put on the traditional Mediterranean black mourning dress—and seldom took it off thereafter.

A twenty-seven-year-old immigrant with two young children—my father, then almost three years old, and one-year-old sister, Fina—Rosalia remarried the year after she was widowed. Her new husband, Samuel Marziano, was in no way the equal of her beloved Antonino. Married before, Samuel was a thirty-four-year-old peddler who owned his own horse and cart and had been naturalized as a U.S. citizen in New York. He lacked Antonino's broad shoulders, square jaw, regular features, fair skin, and alert eyes. A short man, around 5'2", of slender build, olive complexion, with an artificial left eye, he had an erratic temper. When intense, sharp-tongued Rosalia scolded him for touching other women in her presence, he retaliated by hitting her and accusing her of having illicit affairs. One of his blows aimed at Rosalia sent their youngest daughter, Pauline, to the hospital after she tried protecting her mother from him.[26]

Rosalia's thirteen-year marriage to Samuel, which produced three daughters—Josephine (b. 1918), Carmella, known as Milly (b. 1921), and Pauline (b. 1922)—ended abruptly one morning in August 1929. Under Rosalia's questioning, Fina, then fifteen years old, acknowledged that she had had sex the night before with her stepfather. Breaking the stereotype that Sicilian women endure abuse in silence and never make their complaints public, Rosalia, defying all the premises of the notorious Sicilian code of honor, went directly to the nearest police station and accused Samuel of raping their daughter. He was formally charged. Before the trial an official court evalu-

---

[26] Rosemarie Fazekas, cousin, daughter of Pauline Marziano Rizzuto, to the author, January 28, 2004.

ator working through an Italian translator concluded, giving us an unusual document for family history, that Samuel Marziano possessed only borderline intelligence. The report selectively read, as quoted, "Mental Age 5, Intelligence Quotient 3...unstable and impulsive, with certain neurotic tendencies.... Likewise, he appears rather lacking in insight, simple and childish in his judgments and in basic make-up, seems definitely primitive or elemental."[27] At the conclusion of a brief trial, he was found guilty of sexually abusing Fina over the course of a year. He was sentenced to from seven to twenty-five years in prison, of which he served approximately fifteen years.[28]

I saw my step-grandfather, of whom we never spoke, only twice. The first time, when I was about ten years old and he was just recently released from prison, he came for a short visit to my Aunt Pauline's house, where the family was celebrating the baptism of her son. I was with my dad when he approached me in the backyard. After barely a greeting, Samuel gave me a large hunting knife, with a scary long blade and, as I mention in the poem "At the Gate," a hideous purple plastic handle. It was nothing like the leather-handled Boy Scout knife I coveted, and even then, I recognized it was ugly, cheap, and deeply out of place as a gift. The second time I saw Samuel was on Memorial Day a few years later, through the window of our passing car. My parents and I were driving to visit the family graves at Mount Olivet Cemetery. He was standing along the road at one corner of the cemetery, selling small American flags, pinwheels, and other grave decorations. We didn't stop or wave.

Fina, Samuel's hapless victim, was born in 1914, the first year of World War I, and died in 1945, the last year of World War II, sug-

---

[27] Report from Men's Probation Department, Recorder's Court, October 14, 1929, in Recorder's Court of the City of Detroit vs. Samuel Marziano, Case No. 91342, August 1929.

[28] For the transcript of the trial, see City of Detroit vs. Samuel Marziano, Case No. 91342, August 1929.

gesting (as perhaps every family historian must acknowledge) that more than national and world events punctuate a family's history. Considered unfit for marriage to someone of her own age and choosing, Fina married Philip Trupiano, a Sicilian seventeen years her senior. A longtime employee at Chrysler, Phil had an energetic crackly voice, an effusive kindness, and a cunning knack as a card player, who held his pinochle cards in a peacock-like fan. Fina bore no children and died unexpectedly in the course of her first pregnancy from a blood clot that traveled to her brain. Superstitions had presaged her death. Just weeks earlier, my mother, with all the sisters gathered around, announced that she found only a short lifeline on Fina's palm. A month earlier, a reader of tea leaves, called to entertain the members of a tea club, could not decipher a future in the dregs of Fina's cup. And on the day she died yet another omen was given when a bird flew into her house.

At the end of 1929, on the eve of the Great Depression, Rosalia, now forty years old, found herself a divorced widow with five children. She found some support from the families of her brother John (Cruciano) and sister Paulina, who lived nearby, and from certain Beniteau Avenue neighbors, one of whom she always respectfully addressed as *cummare* (godmother) Rosalia Brucato. However, if she and the family were to survive, Rosalia had to count on her seventeen-year-old son, Joe, my father. She recognized his crucial role as the principal wage earner of the family, in effect the man of the house. She gave him his own room and sometimes served him meat, while his four sisters ate the standard fare of pasta, beans, potatoes, and greens. Because Rosalia had always favored her only surviving son, she honored his wish to keep the family together and not put the younger girls in an orphanage, despite the urging of relatives. Rosalia also worked hard to bring in money—as a wet nurse, a laundress, a midwife, and landlady for boarders.

Even though she had completed only two years of schooling in Sicily, Rosalia valued education. She taught herself to read English by poring over the daily newspaper, and she proudly signed her own name on her naturalization papers, instead of scrawling an "X" on the document, as did many other immigrants. At one time, in the early 1920s, she even found money to pay for violin lessons for Joe. Around the same time, when he reported to her that a fellow student at Ford's trade school (where he had just enrolled) had lost a hand, Rosalia insisted that her son immediately withdraw and return to high school; she would not have him sacrifice a limb to industry. Joe rewarded Rosalia's trust by skipping a year and a half of secondary school and graduating with honors at age sixteen. He immediately went to work as a white-collar clerk at Western Union, where he remained hard working and advancing in position for the next forty-three years.

Dad never disappointed my grandmother. Like the eldest child in many immigrant families, he did not shirk the immense responsibility that life had foisted upon him. He embraced his role as father, making sure the family was fed and housed and that the girls always received at least one Christmas gift. He also was adamant that they, too, finish high school. Dedicating a large portion of his salary to the family, he put off getting married until he was twenty-five years old and knew that Rosalia was secure and the girls were mature. In the mid-1930s, he had purchased a house for the family on Hillger Street two blocks east of Beniteau, and after World War II sold it for a modest sum to his stepsister Milly and her husband, Sam Salamagna, stipulating that Rosalia would live with them until she died.

Once her daughters were raised, Rosalia began working as a janitor at nearby Foch Elementary School and remained there for a decade. By the time she retired from that job around age sixty-five and began collecting Social Security benefits, she was worn out and suffering from emphysema. Increasingly, she called on God to spare her any further days here, down below. Teasingly, my mother would caution her that each such entreaty would add a year to her life, but Rosalia continued her supplications. Misery had remained her companion, and complaint, which echoed so discordantly in a 1950s and 1960s America of opportunity, hope, and progress, had become her lifelong habit.

In such profound contrast to my restless American grandmother Frances, *Nunna* Rosalia never questioned who she was, where she had been, and what she could become. And unlike Frances Linsdau, who moved so frequently that I cannot picture her in any one home, I associate Rosalia with the Hillger house. There she reigned supreme from my first memories until I was almost out of high school. Food, its preparation and consumption, centered *Nunna*'s home. At its dining-room table we celebrated all the holidays. The kitchen, with its icebox, on the side of which the young men shot craps, still evokes fond memories. Beans soaked in pots in the closets and in the bathtub. Once, to my and my cousin Angela's glee, snails escaped the kitchen sink and slithered up the walls and across the ceiling. Like many other immigrants to America, Grandma Amato kept a small garden of greens in the backyard in front of the garage, which held stepfather Samuel's cart and horse from which my dad, only a boy of seven, sold fruit. Rosalia delighted in recounting how my father had once caught a wild rabbit in the backyard and how the family then feasted on it. In the musty basement were chicken cages and a wine barrel. My grandmother knew how to wring a chicken's neck, with a twirl, then scald off its feathers, and prepare it for eating. A two-foot-long box of spaghetti was stored under her bed, which cousin Angel and I turned into "swords," which I ate after they snapped off in battle.

My grandmother animated the household, and we cringed in the face of her stern defense of the living room and its furniture. But after every scolding, she compensated me—her only grandson, the only child of her only surviving son, born of her first husband—with hugs and money. During the nights I stayed at her house, I would snuggle up next to her to sleep. She would recount the following morning, to my joy, how I tossed and turned and kicked all night long.

Nunna seemed most happy when she accompanied us on our Sunday excursions into the countryside, which provided opportunities to buy fresh fruit and reminisce about the bountiful harvests of Sicily. She also enjoyed our trips to northern Michigan with her beloved son, Joe, his wife, Ethel (whom she called Etella), and me. Sometimes she became almost as giddy as a child. Once, when my parents hired a buggy for us to tour Mackinaw Island, my grandmother and I sat up front, directly behind the driver and his farting horse. With each step, there was a fart; with each fart, a giggle, and then mounting chuckles that cascaded into contagious and uncontrollable laughter. The Fort Mackinaw and the Grand Hotel—it seemed the whole island itself shook with the hilarity.

Near the end of her life a brief trip to the Italian grocery sufficed to reinvigorate Rosalia. It was as if she had returned to the first true love and ultimate necessity of her life, food. But for all the times I saw her happy—dancing at a wedding, for example—I more often saw her sad. I remember her happily bustling in her kitchen, but I also recall her walking slowly and painfully out of Foch Elementary School. (One day, she happened to board a bus I was riding but did not see me; and it took several minutes before I recognized the short, worn-down woman as my grandmother.) She complained how difficult it was for her to climb a ladder and clean the windows, but she relished telling how a big snake escaped from its case in a science classroom and how she and a fellow janitress feared all day that it would reappear. I think of her, especially now that I am in my seventies, sitting in the back row of De Santis's Funeral Home for hours with the other old women dressed in black—talking, remembering, reviewing lives, and crying about stories that crossed oceans and went to the heart of families.

FROM VILLAGE TO DETROIT, FROM SICILY TO AMERICA, AND BACK

My father's sense of responsibility for the living and dead and my mother's incessant story collecting and repeating set me afloat in memory and history. My grandparents were a ship of flesh into the past. *Nunna* Rosalia furnished a stern rudder to my youthful buoyancy. More than offering anecdotes and proverbs, Rosalia, with the full gravity of her life, shaped my imagination and conscience, which are indispensable for all migrants crossing from deep peasant to contemporary times.

Entering Rosalia's world, if only in memory, plunges me into a remote time and place where work, pain, and death ruled everyday life. As close as I was to her, we were worlds apart in terms of experience. I, who spent so much time at play and sport, belonged to a generation and society distinguished by freedom, optimism, and choice, while she, on the other hand, came from a world dominated by necessity, fate, and mortality. Her kind pulled the blocks for the Egyptian pyramids, plowed fields without horse or mule, suffered the weather, the hunger, the famine, and the lord. I began to sense the tragic nature of her life when I was old enough to recognize the tragic nature of life itself. She contradicted the facile consolation of faith and optimism. Knowing her, I did not assimilate assurances and visions of long life and certain progress. Long before she died, the graveyard (*il camposanto*) had a hold of her. Antonino stood ahead, waiting, holding open the golden gate.

After ten years of pain and loneliness, when she was seventy-seven years old, in 1964, death finally kept its rendezvous. Daughter Milly and new husband, Dale, had moved Rosalia from the old neighborhood to the east side of Detroit, near the city limits. Wearied by age, sequestered by circumstances, and weighed down by leaden memories, Rosalia seemed quite ready to die. She often bruised the feelings of gentle, good-natured Milly with Mount Etna-like emotional explosions. Visits from the relatives, trips to the Italian grocery, and an occasional wedding or funeral weren't enough to stave off her constant petitions to God for a prompt death. In her final hours, when I stood vigil down the hall at the hospital, I, too, prayed that her belabored breathing would stop. She had journeyed far from ancient Sicily and the center of the Mediterranean. As the rural poor everywhere, she deserved a refreshing sleep that would erase *la miseria* and reunite her, dancing, with her Antonino. And if only one day, we could join in.

ABOUT THE AUTHOR

JOSEPH A. AMATO is a noted teacher, public speaker, scholar, and author of more than twenty books. He is a retired history professor at Southwest Minnesota State University, where he helped found and chaired the History and Social Sciences Department and directed the Center for Rural and Regional Studies. He is a leading practitioner in the fields of intellectual and cultural history, and local and regional history, where he is an innovator in understanding place and the transformation of everyday life.

The recipient of many honors for his writing and work in history and the humanities, Amato reviews regularly for the *Journal of Social History*. Among his many books are *When Father and Son Conspire: A Minnesota Farm Murder* (1988), *Victims and Values: A History and A Theory of Suffering* (1990); *The Great Jerusalem Artichoke Circus: The Buying and Selling of the Rural American Dream* (1993), *The Decline of Rural Minnesota* (1993), *Rethinking Home: A Guide to Writing Local and Regional History* (2000), *Dust: A History of the Small and Invisible* (2000), *On Foot: A History of Walking* (2007), *Surfaces: A History* (2013), his first collection of poetry, *Buoyancies: A Ballast Master's Log* (2014), and, most recently, *The Book of Twos* (2015). With a forthcoming work on the history of everyday life, *Everyday Life: A Short History its Long and Extraordinary Making,* here Amato returns to a standing interest in family, migration, ethnicity, and his Sicilian-American roots.

Bordighera Press is an imprint of Bordighera, Incorporated, an independently owned not-for-profit
scholarly organization that has no legal affiliation with the University of Central Florida or with
The John D. Calandra Italian American Institute, Queens College/CUNY.

JOHN CASEY, et al. *Imagining Humanity.* Vol. 25. Interdisciplinary Studies. $18

ROBERT LIMA. *Sardinia/Sardegna.* Vol. 24. Poetry. $10

DANIELA GIOSEFFI. *Going On.* Vol. 23. Poetry. $10

ROSS TALARICO. *The Journey Home.* Vol. 22. Poetry. $12

EMANUEL DI PASQUALE. *The Silver Lake Love Poems.* Vol. 21. Poetry. $7

JOSEPH TUSIANI. *Ethnicity.* Vol. 20. Poetry. $12

JENNIFER LAGIER. *Second Class Citizen.* Vol. 19. Poetry. $8

FELIX STEFANILE. *The Country of Absence.* Vol. 18. Poetry. $9

PHILIP CANNISTRARO. *Blackshirts.* Vol. 17. History. $12

LUIGI RUSTICHELLI. Ed.. *Seminario sul racconto.* Vol. 16. Narrative. $10

LEWIS TURCO. *Shaking the Family Tree.* Vol. 15. Memoirs. $9

LUIGI RUSTICHELLI, Ed. *Seminario sulla drammaturgia.* Vol. 14. Theater/Essays. $10

FRED GARDAPHÈ. *Moustache Pete is Dead! Long Live Moustache Pete!.* Vol. 13. Oral Literature.
$10

JONE GAILLARD CORSI. *Il libretto d'autore.* 1860–1930. Vol. 12. Criticism. $17

HELEN BAROLINI. *Chiaroscuro: Essays of Identity.* Vol. 11. Essays. $15

PICARAZZI & FEINSTEIN, Eds. *An African Harlequin in Milan.* Vol. 10. Theater/Essays. $15

JOSEPH RICAPITO. *Florentine Streets & Other Poems.* Vol. 9. Poetry. $9

FRED MISURELLA. *Short Time.* Vol. 8. Novella. $7

NED CONDINI. *Quartettsatz.* Vol. 7. Poetry. $7

ANTHONY JULIAN TAMBURRI, Ed. *Fuori: Essays by Italian/American Lesbians and Gays.* Vol. 6.
Essays. $10

ANTONIO GRAMSCI. P. Verdicchio. Trans. & Intro. *The Southern Question.* Vol. 5. Social
Criticism. $5

DANIELA GIOSEFFI. *Word Wounds & Water Flowers.* Vol. 4. Poetry. $8

WILEY FEINSTEIN. *Humility's Deceit: Calvino Reading Ariosto Reading Calvino.* Vol. 3.
Criticism. $10

PAOLO A. GIORDANO, Ed. *Joseph Tusiani: Poet. Translator. Humanist.* Vol. 2. Criticism. $25

ROBERT VISCUSI. *Oration Upon the Most Recent Death of Christopher Columbus.* Vol. 1. Poetry.
$3